Penguin Science Fiction

SPLIT SECOND

Evacuated from London during the bombing, Garry Kilworth's mother produced him in York in 1941. His parents were travellers, and his teenage years were spent in southern Arabia.

After two years at an Air Force technical college, he was sent to Malaya and Singapore. He also spent a year on a tiny coral island, one of the Maldives in the Indian Ocean. He later spent prolonged periods of time in Germany, Africa, Bahrain, Aden, Malta and Cyprus. It was during those years, in fact, that he began to write fiction and poetry, and in 1974 he won the Gollancz/*Sunday Times* Science Fiction competition.

He is now a Senior Telecommunications Executive with a communications firm that operates on a world-wide basis. Apart from communications and writing, he enjoys the family activities of canoeing, camping in the wilds, ornithology and collecting anything of no use to nature or Man. He is married to a social worker and they have two teenage children.

Garry Kilworth's other novels, *In Solitary* and *The Night of Kadar*, are also published in Penguins.

GARY KILWORTH

SPLIT SECOND

Penguin Books

Penguin Books Ltd, Harmondsworth, Middlesex, England
Penguin Books, 625 Madison Avenue, New York, New York 10022, U.S.A.
Penguin Books Australia Ltd, Ringwood, Victoria, Australia
Penguin Books Canada Ltd, 2801 John Street, Markham, Ontario, Canada L3R 1B4
Penguin Books (N.Z.) Ltd, 182–190 Wairau Road, Auckland 10, New Zealand

First published by Faber & Faber 1979
Published in Penguin Books 1981

Printed and bound in Great Britain by
Cox & Wyman Ltd, Reading

For Ray, who is more than a brother

Acknowledgements

My thanks to Marshall, Sutton Ltd. and compiler Robin Parker, producers of 'Aphrodite's Realm', and to the people of Cyprus for whom I developed considerable respect during my years on that ancient island. My thanks also to Andrew Stephenson for the energy brick calculations and to Judy Monk for the hand-drawn map of Cyprus.

Man is a little wind that lilts the air,
And passing, leaves no shadow there,
But I, beside him when his days are flown
Take back my own to be my own . . .

Len Kendall, 'The Creator'

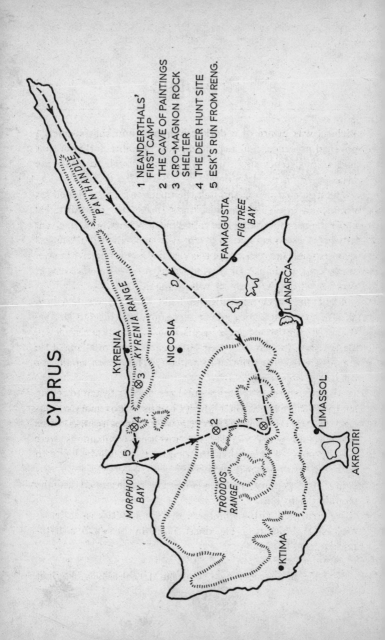

CYPRUS

1 NEANDERTHALS'
  FIRST CAMP
2 THE CAVE OF PAINTINGS
3 CRO-MAGNON ROCK
  SHELTER
4 THE DEER HUNT SITE
5 ESK'S RUN FROM RENG.

PANHANDLE

KYRENIA   *KYRENIA RANGE*

⊗3

⊗4

5

MORPHOU BAY

⊗2

⊗1

TROODOS RANGE

NICOSIA

FAMAGUSTA

FIG TREE BAY

LANARCA

LIMASSOL

AKROTIRI

KTIMA

Prologue

Richard was aware of a darkness around him that seemed a physical presence, not just an absence of light: darkness that had a consistency like thick fog, dense enough to obliterate even the brightest sun's rays.

He struggled to see through the opaqueness that filmed his vision and gradually the blackness turned to grey mist. He could sense something close to his head. A breathing, like that of a pet dog waking him from a heavy sleep? His head? He was inside something; of that he was certain. A container. A tank of some kind, perhaps? Or a windowless room? No, he knew it was a head, and he, Richard, was on the inside.

Panic rushed through his mind like a strong wind. A boy, shrunk to the size of a mouse and squeezed through an eye-socket — imprisoned in a fossil! One of his father's ancient skulls, that was it! He tried to scream, but could make no sound. He had lost control of his body. The mouth would not open. The eyes would not see.

After a period of terrifying mind-screams he began to regain sanity. Richard was a loner, always had been. Rosemary was his one occasional companion. His own company was often enough and when younger the invented companions were usually more exciting than the real ones. Slowly he came to realize he was trapped somewhere. He could escape only by using his ingenuity; running down the corridors of insanity wouldn't help him.

He struggled with his limbless, eyeless, mouthless, earless — earless? He *could* hear. He concentrated on the sound, a rhythmic grunted breathing.

"Uhuh! Uhuh! Uhuh!"

At least he was not deaf. And the darkness *was* clearing;

drifting away. He forced his mind forward, trying to penetrate the fog before it.

> The eyes are for seeing,
> The ears for hearing,
> The mouth for . . .

Someone was there beside him, in the head. That was his, the Other's breath, heaving in and out of the mouth below the mind. Richard wanted to ask a name, then realized he was being sidetracked. Forget the other mind, use your own! Wait. Why bypass? Why not connect? It was possible, he could feel the pressure of the other person against himself. Open out. Let him in.

Suddenly, Richard could see.

1

The granite moved in the near dawn: an igneous rock stirring from an ageless sleep. It lifted its head to the skyline, as yet only a red grimace separating the dark air from the darker sea. Below the head the rock took on the tense form and shape of a man's torso, limbs appeared, and hair was shaken around the heavy shoulders.

The granite man then rose on colonnade legs, moving towards the growing mouth of the morning, out of the shrinking throat of the cave.

Granla, Shaman of the Gren, went to greet the Mother, Her belly as silent as it had been on the third day of the creation.

"Mother of the wind," he began. "Of the trees like hair upon your form; of the lesser sea mother; the ice-eye and the fire-eye that give us light, and all the beasts that run across your back like the fleas of my head – give a good hunt today. Your children need food." He moved his hands with the eloquence of the words, shaping the trees and the animals in the air, running extended fingers over his forearm to show the Mother he knew the rippling beauty of life-sustaining water.

Returning to the rock shelter, which was almost a cave in its depth, he found his deerskins and pulled them on. Outside the small circle of night fires the world was a peninsula of ice and snow – at the top was the snow, and low down, around the beaches, a frost waxed and waned depending upon the time of day. The Great Ice Age encompassed Granla and his group like a cold ring of stone. It tightened around the big man's chest as he went out in the half-darkness, towards the place where a thin rope of water fell twisting from the rocks above.

As he walked he kicked bodies awake. Some, lumps of clay that merely groaned and rolled – others, the young ones, lithe

13

saplings that sprang back into place after a night's enforcement into unnatural postures. They rose and moved with the Shaman towards the water. Mnemonic mountains grew before their eyes as they shambled, and grass and trees they had known before their sleep reminded them that they were men, spawned by the Mother. Each one mumbled his own individual orisons as he walked, the journey ending in a sweet drink of freezing water.

As they drank in turns and took away the slime or roughness from their throats they started to chatter. The birds had already begun their oral demarcation and, while some beasts rose from warm beds of leaves to enter the day, others were exiting to artificial nights in woodwork, earthwork or stone hollow.

"The women should have the morning food ready by now," said Berfas. Someone replied, "If you could throw a spear as well as you do your tongue, none of us would want for food."

"None but you," Berfas snapped back, "for if the meat fell under my spear, your share would be the hoofs."

"Listen to the great rabbit hunter – you would think by now he would know his prey had paws."

The men laughed and Berfas spat disgustedly.

Spasmodic sounds of chinking stone, activity and hissing wood found their ears as they returned. Granla returned to the mouth of the rock shelter, to where his own fire blew out its white breath into the chill air.

"Some meat," he ordered of his two women. "Meat and the juice of fruits."

He looked with pride over his kingdom – the thickly forested slopes below the mountains, that fell onto a rocky shoreline and thence into the sea. There were rare clearings in the forest where whalebacks of gneiss broke the surface of the dew-decked world to slide, black and shining, slowly down into earth again. Streams turned over onto their dorsal humps to reveal white vulnerable bellies of foam, and fell with opened legs from high cliffs into the sea. Birds drew spirals, beasts crawled along crooked paths of their own making. This was his

14

kingdom – not perfect, for there was a lack of flint, though some could be found, and chalcedony and malachite served almost as well – but as near to perfect as the sea was to the sky. It was difficult not to acknowledge the pride of ownership filling his chest.

Suddenly, out of the corner of his eyes, Granla caught sight of a single sleeping form.

Esk was awakened after the sun. Where as the fire-eye had a slow, gentle rising, Esk was lifted violently by his hair and set jarringly on his feet. At sixteen – almost middle age – he was unused to such indignities.

"Arghh!" he yelled, more in anger than in pain. Being fresh from sleep his anger was naturally instantaneous and more vehement than was normal for him, and he swung to bite the wrist above his long black mane. Granla cuffed him heavily as his teeth snapped at thin air.

"Ungrateful youth," growled the broad-chested giant. "It's your food-hunting day. Why didn't you rise with the fire-eye and speak to the Mother of all things for a good hunt?"

Esk's anger waned swiftly. He was lucky that it had not been Reng that had found him. Reng was his half-brother – older and stronger. He would have driven his heel into Esk's soft-asleep stomach.

"I'm going, Granla. I'm going. I was whispering to the grass."

"Lying youth," said Granla, but Esk was one of his favourites and he did not strike him a second time.

Esk took up his spear, muttering in an aggrieved tone, "I was speaking with the Mother, in my sleep. I heard Her talking back to my ears in the dark."

The night before he had lain in the entrance to the rock shelter listening to the grasses sighing and calling his name. He had fallen asleep, answering them softly. Esk was convinced he was a special youth, chosen by the Mother to perform great deeds. One day he would move the world with his strength.

He slipped away from the shelf and down the worn path into

the undergrowth, hastily chanting the prayers he should have said just before the dawn.

". . . may the Mother be childful," he finished, coming out of the trees at the edge of the beach. The other youths would already be out and perhaps had made their kills. Some of them, the ones that disliked hunting, would be climbing for birds' eggs. It was the job of the youths to supply certain midday meals. Each had to bring home enough to feed the women, the infirm and the very young attached to him by his birth. Esk had two young sisters and his mother and grandmother to feed. His younger and older brothers would have to find their own food. Tomorrow it would be his younger brother, Slek, that would feed the women and sisters and Esk would only need to feed himself.

Running along the beach, his feet making deep prints in the sand at the waterline, Esk's intention was to try for a large wading bird with his spear. The birds were quick to sense a man and he would need a place where the edge of the trees grew close to the sea mother. Within a spear's throw if possible. Such a spot was a good long run along the flat beach but it was a cold morning and the youth was glad to have exercise which would warm him. Clad in a loose singlet and shorts of deerskin the breeze found the most intimate parts of his body with its icy fingers.

When he reached his hideout Esk settled down for a long wait amongst the wet fronds of a forest floor fern. Joined with the dark woods again he felt secure and peaceful. The earth was his Mother, the trees and the plants Her fond arms and hands wrapping themselves around his boulder-hard body. In Her were all the creatures of the world, from the tiniest beetle to the great spear-toothed giants that sometimes came in from the outside. (Granla said the giants slid down from the sky on the shining paths of the ice-eye at night, for why would the Mother Herself make creatures She could not hide in Her clothes. They were easy to find because they stood tall above the bushes – but they fought and killed in madness, crushing men to death with one stamp of a foot.)

16

Esk was close to the Mother. She had never tried to hurt him. One of the other youths had been the target for Her displeasure and was now under a rockfall.

As he lay in his warm nest of leaves, waiting for the shore birds to move nearer to the trees, Esk suddenly sensed danger nearby. Or was it? Possibly a wolf or savage cat had wandered by earlier and left its scent near the ferns. The youth sniffed. Not the scent of a dangerous beast. Certainly smells were there. They always hung lightly in the breeze or were strong amongst the roots of the grasses. But each one could be identified individually and none seemed bad to him. Why then his uneasiness?

There! Strong. A fire-smoke scent. Not really near, perhaps some several runs distant. Not the camp. That was down-wind. Coming from the thin land that went out like a woman's arm into the sea mother?

Esk forgot his hunt and began running for high ground, wanting to see where the smoke was coming from. Perhaps some of the other youths had run away and were making fire a long way off? They would be beaten if they were caught because Granla would only allow a fire at the entrance to the shelter, well away from the trees. Fires were ordered to life, or extinguished, by Granla and no one else. They killed swiftly if allowed to roam free and scarred the Mother's face.

He reached rocks above the trees and stared for a long time over the milk-mistiness of the forest roof. No smoke could be seen rising from the thinner vapour and Esk began to feel he might have been mistaken. A trick by the Mother, perhaps, to test Her offspring. Not all things were explained by the senses. Some things were unreal. They came and went, like ghosts with no substance. Esk's eyes were for seeing and true to him.

The Mother turned Her belly slowly under the fire-eye, like a giant spear-tooth rolling over in death, but the young ones would be getting hungry. Esk crouched, ready to slide down the slope into the trees again when something caught his eye. A thin wisp of smoke, thinner than a thread, a long way off.

Immediately he saw, his legs began to move, running him in

17

the direction of the rock shelter. The Mother aided his progress, throwing his feet forward from Her sponge-moss belly.

On reaching the rock shelter he shouted for the Shaman. Women crowded round him as he strode breathless to Granla's *place*. His woman said, "Hunting. My man is hunting."

Reng stamped up to his half-brother, loudly demanding to know the news.

"Take me to Granla," was all Esk would say. "Take me to the Shaman." He would not hand over his precious news to Reng no matter what happened.

For once Reng would have to take a share of any glory that was available, and not steal it all for himself.

"Follow me," he said, snatching an available antler-tipped spear, and began trotting up the slope behind the rock shelf with Esk on his heels. One or two of the men followed the youths.

Reng was the best tracker in the group and he paused only for a second at each fork or crosspath before moving on. A sniff, a touch, and Granla's track was known to Reng. The boys were fast and before long had left the two men behind. Finally, they broke into a clearing where Granla and the rest of the hunters were standing and conversing after failing to kill their quarry.

"Granla," shouted Esk. "Someone comes from the Far Place."

The search for the blame for losing the deer ceased abruptly.

"Who comes?" asked Granla.

"I do not know. I saw the smoke of their fire."

They clustered around Esk and Reng, questioning both youths until it was obvious that only conjecture could follow Esk's first statement. A fast runner was then despatched towards the newcomers' camp with instructions to return unseen by them.

The next morning the runner returned, exhausted. A new group was coming, he said, but not like the men of the Gren. They were small, square people with heavy faces and there were many of them, said the runner – a great many.

2

Paul Levan carefully brushed the sandy soil away from the object with trembling fingers, his heavy-boned hand inept at a task which required a more delicate touch. He could have used the blower, or even the soft lens brush, but he had yearned so long for this moment that he was not going to be robbed of the sensation of uncovering the beautiful lines with his own finger-tips.

"Beautiful" was not an adjective everyone would have used to describe the piece of bone resting in his palm, but Levan was an amateur archaeologist, and this particular strip of dead human tissue represented a rise in the ranks of that select band of men who are rich enough to be able to dabble in such time-consuming pursuits. He had found his first human.

Possibly he was excited for no reason. The two inches of lower jawbone in his fingers might have come from a relatively recent occupant of the Earth. He would soon know. If it was human, what then? What, he thought, what *kind* of human? *Homo sapiens sapiens? Homo sapiens neanderthalensis?* He did not mind which, so long — just so long — as it was over 30,000 years old. The "dawn of man", *Homo erectus*, was too much to hope for. God no, he would be too tempted to use the cliché in his paper. Better the "dusk of man". Or some such phrase. A tinge of humour, yet serious. A confirmation of his earlier findings in the same location: the flint tools, already layer-dated at around 35,000 years, give or take a few thousand.

Placing the mandible carefully in a plastic bag he then folded a neckerchief around the package. He should have brought a box, he thought, but then how did he know he would find anything today? And what size of box? He had not, in fact,

19

intended to dig today. Richard had wanted a swim and he had brought the boy here, below the site in the Kyrenia mountains. "Don't fool yourself Levan," he said quietly. "You knew you'd dig if you came within a thousand yards of the place."

No box then. He slipped it into the pocket of his safari jacket. The mark of the professional was to be poorly equipped anyway. Only rich amateurs loaded themselves and their hired help with expensive instruments, analysing rods and velvet-lined carrying baskets. Paul Levan hated being taken for what he was. He liked being the small boy fishing with a stick and bent pin.

Levan looked down the wooded slopes to the beach by Snake Island. The boy was still swimming with seemingly limit-less energy; practising for a school gala. Paul Levan called to his son.

"Rick! . . . Richard," he bawled the second time.

No answer. The wind was against him. An onshore breeze. He had wanted to show the boy the exact spot. Arouse some interest for the father's hobby in the son. It would have to be later, though, and Richard had not yet been bitten by the bug. He was polite enough, but it was the distant politeness of a fourteen-year-old, wanting to please, yet desperate to be with his peers. Since there was no longer a mother, the man and the youth needed company and seldom antagonized each other.

Levan began to walk over the rocky ground and down towards the beach. It was spring in Cyprus and the sun beat hotly on his thick neck, exposed now without the kerchief. Around him the green of the winter undergrowth had already begun to turn to the brittle, tawny hues of summer. Thorns crouched beneath his bootsoles, then sprang up again in his wake, and dry grasses whispered like paper at the touch of his slacks. Soon the brushwood would be full of noisy ticking insects – or at least the insects would be more evident upon the scrubland. Local Cypriots would set fire to the fields and hills in order to drive them away, often succeeding only in herding the pests into their own gardens and kitchens. The giant grass-hopper on the bathroom cabinet would return the morning

stare until the intruder was recognized and became the pro-
voker of female screams.

The sleek-looking slider was at the roadside where Levan had
left it. Even with wheel-less vehicles it was still safer to use the
roads. Being a Lather-Sneiman, Levan's slider was of course
equipped with sweepers but half-buried rocks take time to
shift and if the vehicle is travelling at speed the sweepers might
not have time to do their job effectively. The roads and beaches
carried most of the traffic in backwaters like Cyprus and at
least the sliders obviated the need for highway maintenance.

Opening the slider hatch Levan deposited his precious package inside the vehicle, then he locked the hatch again and
strode across the dirt sand, stained by the cigarette ash of
several million tourists long before Levan's time, to where his
son was wallowing in the Mediterranean. Some things never
change, thought Levan. The sea is constant. The peasant with
the donkey, further down the beach, will always be there in
one form or another. The shanty dwellings change little
through the ages. Only the rich benefited from the advance-
ments in science and technology the late twentieth century
could offer. It was a measure of the success of the human race
that the poor became fewer. Or did they? Perhaps they merely
died and were slow to be replaced? Were there still cave dwell-
ers on the earth, even now?

"Dreaming again, Dad?"

Levan jerked his bare head upright to see a lean youth, long
dark hair plastered to his head and shoulders, holding out his
hands for a towel.

"Don't give me that, boy, I'm going to be a famous man," he
drawled, slightly annoyed at being so transparent, even to a
fourteen-year-old, and attempting to hide it under a mock
countryman accent.

The towel was handed over – or rather thrown and caught –
with easy grace on both sides. Levan was glad they were not
too far apart in years to appreciate each other physically.
Emma and he had had the boy when they were young.

Richard rubbed furiously at his thick mop of hair and then

21

slipped into his shorts with his wet trunks still on, making damp patches appear on the already salt-stained cloth.

"You'll catch cold," said Levan, mostly to himself. It was too warm for that. He was considering the slider seatcovers more than his son's state of health. Richard had not even bothered to answer.

They walked back across the hot sand to the slider, Richard's sandals throwing up small clouds behind his heels, and were soon slipping through the fir tree groves and up the slope between Bellapais Abbey and St Hilarion Castle towards the pass to Nicosia.

"Where are we going?" asked Richard.

Their rented bungalow was in Bellapais and he had been looking forward to an evening lazing around on the balcony. Sometimes his father gave him a glass of beer, which was fast becoming the prime nutrient in his life.

"We're going to the labs. I want to get something checked out."

Richard could see the colour rising in his father's face and he guessed that the old man had found something on his site.

"Okay, pop. What did you find?" He used a resigned tone, as if he knew he would have to suffer a lecture soon, so might as well get it over with. Paul flushed a deeper red.

"Well . . . you don't really want to hear do you? I'll only bore the hell out of you."

"You'll tell me anyway."

Paul was serious. "No, no . . . you'll hear, because it's big, but I'm not going to tell you . . . not if you're going to take that 'Okay, I'll bear him' attitude."

Richard laughed, enjoying the game, although he knew he could only carry it so far before his father would start becoming properly annoyed.

They were in open countryside now. Farmland. Levan cut a corner, sliding a few inches above the carefully prepared and seeded ground. Cyprus was a backward country. They still depended upon their crops to a certain extent, although there was one plankton farm out in the sea, offshore from Paphos.

"I found a piece of skull," Levan said suddenly.

"Stim!" snapped back Richard, caught unawares and using the latest catchword to express heavy approval. It was not the find that interested him, but the word "skull" flung at him like that. Paul was good at impressing people, even those that knew him well.

"A piece of jawbone."

"Yeah? What does that mean . . .? Anyway, I found a part of a skull, too, on the beach."

Levan looked at his son quickly.

"Where? What?" he asked, thinking *it might match.* Boy and father find *Kyrenia Man.*

"Here," said Richard, holding open an empty palm. Levan looked puzzled and Richard added, "It's an eye socket . . . see?" He formed a ring with his thumb and forefinger.

For an instant Levan felt deeply disappointed. "That's no joke . . ." he started to say, but then realized it was and tried to grin.

"Anyway, it might be big — this jawbone thing," he said. "Could be quite a find. Not much else that old has been found in Cyprus. Plenty later — the beehive cultures. But no Cro-Magnon."

"How do you know?"

"How do I know what?" he asked, thinking the boy was about to question his knowledge of other "finds".

"How do you know it's the Cro-Magnon era?"

"Oh." Richard was right. He shouldn't count on the mandible fragment being as old as the artifacts he had found. It was possible they didn't match. No. No. They were both at the same level. This time he was sure. Not like that time in France with Emma. God, those erotic cave drawings! Emma. Gone now. Now it was Lorrie.

He answered the boy's question.

"I'm only guessing, but it's an educated guess. We'll know soon enough. We'll have it radiocarbon dated first. Then, if

23

that's positive – I mean, if the bone is old enough to warrant it, we'll have it M-screened. . . ."

"That's the newest technique isn't it? I heard you telling Loraine last week."

Levan gave a heavy sigh. "Not *quite* the latest, son."

They were nearing Limassol now and the roads and verges were beginning to fill with vehicles, nudging each other with their magnetic repellent fields.

"Well, what *is* the latest? If you hadn't wanted me to ask you wouldn't have mentioned it."

"The Wiederhaus Repeater process."

"What?"

"Phantoms. It's a mirror to reflect the past."

Richard snorted. "Stim! Ghosts? You mean you can make ghosts out of that piece of bone?"

Levan suddenly thought: Damn. Probably not. Maybe it'd take more than just the small piece he had already.

"Not really ghosts. A man named Wiederhaus claims he can reproduce a picture of the original provided the bone is authentic."

Coincidentally they were passing beneath the massive solar screens that robbed St Andrew's shopping complex of most of its sunlight.

"It takes a lot of power, though," he added. "It's a three-dimensional reproduction. Impressive, I'm told. But very expensive."

"Never mind, pop," said the blissfully ignorant boy beside him. "You're loaded with the stuff. Get it out of the bank." With that Richard's attention was gone. Lost somewhere in the crowd milling around the brightly fronted shops. It's a pity, thought Levan, that purses are not as infinite as the young believe them to be. He was wealthy all right, and he could afford the process. But it would knock a huge hole in his fortune and he had to be certain first. Levan senior had made the future by getting in early on processing grass and deciduous leaves into food. Now Levan junior was about to unmake it by processing a piece of a dead man's jaw into a transitory glimpse of the original owner. Was it worth it? The old guy would shuffle the ashes in his urn if he knew.

Later that evening he told Loraine what he was about to do, expecting scorn and a rebuke. He had left the bone at the government laboratories, intending that a radiocarbon test should be carried out. He had not the skill or knowledge to do the job himself so he paid others to do it. He was the donkey, or the mole if you like. Digging up the stuff for the experts to play with.

"You know what you want to do. Are you expecting me to tell you you're right?" said Loraine. She was five years older than Levan, just over forty, with tinted dark red hair and a well-preserved figure. The breasts sagged a little when they were without their supports, but Levan did not find that unbecoming. He liked it. They had met through their children, who were in the same class at a Famagusta school.

"I can't tell you how to spend your own money, Paul."

"No," he replied, "but everyone needs advice – no matter who they are, or what they intend to do. I often wonder how God manages – but then I suppose if you look around you at the mess, you see that he doesn't. . . ."

"Don't blaspheme," she said, tight-lipped. "Anyway, what you want is confirmation, not advice. Alan wasn't like you, a little boy. He didn't need support." It was a lie she often repeated, he thought. Her eyes were hard. The weakness of men did not seem to endear them to her. Why was it, then, thought Levan, that she was always attracted to the same sort of man? Yet when she had him, she seemed to suffer so much. She seldom smiled.

"Where's Rosemary?" he asked, to change the subject, knowing that Loraine's daughter would be in bed.

"She's out dancing with a middle-aged man. Oh, don't be foolish," she added when he pulled a face. "Where did you think she was? I sent her to bed two hours ago."

They were sitting on the balcony and he put his arm around

25

the back of her chair and under her hair. He felt her stiffen as his fingers touched the fine hair on the nape of her neck.

"Stars are out," he said.

"And am I supposed to melt now, because of that?" she said, exaggerating her soft anglicized Scots accent.

"No, you don't have to melt. I like you whatever your chemical state — gas, liquid, solid . . ."

"Alan's written to me," she said, brushing his arm away and taking a sip of brandy from the glass in her hand.

Levan stiffened. "What does *he* want?"

"Well, I am his wife."

"*Were* — you're divorced."

"He's still Rosemary's father. He's talking about coming back. Says . . ."

"I'm not interested in what he says," snapped Levan angrily. "I know why he's coming back — or at least why he talks about it."

There was a warning light in her eyes.

"Tell me why Paul."

He took no heed of the signals.

"Because he's heard about me — knows I've got money. I expect he feels that you're worth me paying out to hold onto. . . ."

"And am I Paul? He wouldn't, heaven forbid, be interested in his wife — as a woman? That would be too far-fetched of course."

Her tone was scathing. Levan was always making the same sort of mistakes with her and he usually finished by apologizing. This time he was annoyed enough to attack.

For once he said the right thing.

"He hasn't bothered to interest himself the last nine years, Lorrie. Don't be greedy. You can't win them all. I love you, he doesn't. You'd have a hell of a time if both of us were hanging round your neck, you have enough trouble coping with just me. . . ."

She was quiet for a while then, "Don't call me Lorrie," was all she said. "My name's Loraine."

26

He knew then how the evening would end.

Later that night, covered only by a sheet and the beginnings of a humid summer they pressed together for security.

"What about the boy?" murmured Loraine.

"Richard? Oh, I see," he said, as he realized why she was asking. "I'll go back to the bungalow before he wakes. I'm not going to sleep anyway."

She snorted. "Don't think that goes both ways because I need to rest. . . ."

"I wasn't thinking. . . . I'm too excited to sleep – the find, I mean. I need to think about it."

"Ugh . . . I'm sticking to you. You're very sweaty tonight. Are you really serious about using most of your money just to prove a point?" She was up on one elbow, looking at him intently in the half-light.

"I might get some of it back again, if I'm right, from the Cyprus government," he replied in a faraway voice, as if he were trying to convince himself. Then, more sure of his ground, he continued, "You see, under the United World rules Cyprus only has island status – a weak position when it comes to claiming a share of the funds. Britain, on the other hand, can claim continental status because she can prove that she was once a part of the mainland. I think I can prove that Cyprus was once joined to the continent by a narrow strip of land, the tail of which is now the panhandle on the north-east . . ."

"Pangaea."

"What?"

"Once upon a time all the Earth's landmass was one great continent; therefore all countries should be able to claim equal status."

"Pangaea is still supposition. They don't *know*. . . . You have to be able to prove, beyond reasonable doubt."

She was tenacious. "What about boats then? They could have crossed by raft."

"Unlikely. It's quite a distance. It's also a fact that the Ice Age robbed the seas of their present depth. The ridge between

27

Tangier and Gibraltar was above sea level, forming a wall across the mouth of the Mediterranean. The Med would not be as deep then, anyway – it's been fed by rivers over a long, long period of time.

"There's something else. Another way I shall retrieve my money." His voice had quietened because he thought she would not approve.

"Private collectors will pay to own prehistoric men. They'll pay a lot for artifacts too – stone spearheads, things like that – but the real money is in skeletons, the older the better. Paleolithic – Upper Paleolithic – men fetch a high price though, because they are the first *real* men. Usually whole skeletons can be found as well – they buried their dead rather than let the animals and elements scatter the bones. *Australopithecus, Homo erectus* – usually incomplete. More often than not, just a skull. . . ."

She was staring at him intently.

"My God," she said at last, in an incredulous tone. "How the rich spread their wealth." She gave a hollow laugh. "Stamp collections, paintings, silver, antiques – those I can understand – but old bones? What do they *do* with them? Sit them in living-room chairs as conversation pieces? Or build museums around them?"

Levan cleared his throat. "Something like that," he said. "The museums, I mean. There are clubs to which they belong – very exclusive. And they have viewings of each other's collections using the Wiederhaus Repeater. It's a harmless hobby . . ."

"Harmless, yes, but the money just flows backwards and forwards between the rich . . ."

"As usual," he finished for her. "Anyway, my main concern is with the discovery of Cyprus as part of the mainland. Any fool with half an eye can see that a landbridge must have existed at one time: the question is, when?" He knew he was gabbling. She stopped him.

"Paul," she said firmly. "Never apologize to me for making money. Previously I thought you were a fool, frittering away your father's fortune – tonight you've shown me that you're as hard-headed a businessman as he ever was. I don't disapprove – I admire you for it. Of course, the idiots that waste their money buying old bones are half-wits. But people like you are different. You exploit the half-wits. That shows common sense."

"God you're a hard woman," said Levan. "Now, about my bridge. . . ."

Loraine smiled. "What about it then?"

He said seriously, "Do *you* believe in it?"

She was quiet for some while, then she said, "Why isn't the ridge, or part of it, there now, below the water – between Cyprus and Turkey I mean." He shrugged and flicked the sheet from him.

"There are places where the water is very shallow – although I admit some areas are more than eighteen fathoms – that's the height the theorists tell us the water has risen since the last Ice Age."

Why had he started this silly conversation? He was making half of it up as he went along anyway.

"Why do you need to? Why bother? – you're not Cypriot."

"I want to . . . because no one else has. As I say, the government will probably recompense, or maybe even reward me. But I don't care very much. I just want the recognition."

"Son of a sausage-maker," she murmured.

Levan heard it but he did not understand. Perhaps it was a private joke of hers because she sighed afterwards – the nearest Loraine ever came to a laugh.

"What?" he asked, guessing he was being made a fool of in some way.

"Sausage-makers, innkeepers, tanners. They toil all their lives to make money, and then pass the fortune on to their sons – who spend *their* lives trying to live down the occupations followed by their fathers. Cleon, the son of a Greek tanner, becomes a politician. Cardinal Wolsey, son of an innkeeper, lord of all England – for a time. . . ."

Levan was amused rather than annoyed.

"Cleon was a merchant-tanner himself. You really ought to brush up on the classical, darling. Besides, my father was in a respectable profession. He didn't get his hands bloody."

She sighed again. "You missed the point. You all feel *guilty* about the money — you, Cleon, Wolsey. You don't want to use it as it is so you try to turn it into *respectable* money. Trying to become somebody in art, or education, or — the worst of all — politics."

"Good," he cried, in mock delight, "so I've got a streak of decency? Education can't be at the very bottom of the slush pile." He nipped her belly lightly.

"Go to hell," she said, rolling over and presenting him with a broad expanse of white bottom. Full moon, he thought. Not my night.

He climbed out of bed, slipped into some shorts and went out on to the balcony. Below him lay the harbour of Kyrenia, little used now that the skipships came right up the slipways and into hangars. The trees were fencing with each other in the light breezes, filling the air with the scent of pine, and he could hear the water licking away at the rocks and sand. It must have been beautiful in those days when men were as rare on the landscape as wolves, he thought. When the food they sought had been as close to them, biologically, as one animal was to another.

The food in big cities was as distant from plants and animals as plastic was from wood. Their sustenance was manufactured from raw chemicals: new life created artificially from basic elements, only to be devoured. The age of the man-god had arrived. Progress?

Sometimes he thought that, instead of moving forwards, they were slipping backwards. What if the progress of Man ended at the point where men began building those famous barriers against the elements? Clothes, houses, cities, walls? Push back the jungles and the seas — make way for Man! What if Aurignac, Solutre or Madeleine people were the apex of the *Homo sapiens*? If men had reached their cultural peak in those times, when simple but exquisitely beautiful art flourished and implements and tools that were shaped from the basic natural earth-kiss-earth stone? If that were true Man was indeed advancing backwards ... backwards towards what? His imagination failed him there. Levan dreamed of past glories. He was no visionary of the future.

He listened to the world growing older for an hour or two and finally the sun rose to scatter its silver rain over the wavelets. The old abbey ruins sucked the light into its dark corners and the lemon-orange trees, those hybrids that grew both fruits from grafted branches, shimmered into shape.

If a mammoth were to come lumbering over the ridge now, thought Levan, it wouldn't surprise me. What was it that one of the American presidents once said on witnessing a particularly tranquil dawn? He called it a Pleistocene day. This is my Pleistocene day, thought Levan. Today I'll find the rest of my Paleolithic Man.

There is a small bay called Fig Tree where, in the season, the pomegranates bleed their blooms, which slowly crystallize to seeds. Where multitudes of tall, fan-bladed wind-pumps await a Messiah to lead them to freedom from their seven-day-a-week toil. Where, over the blue water, skiers repeat the miracle of Galilee at several times the noise, speed and flurry — while Peter, mending his nets, hardly turns his head.

Under the giant fig tree Loraine rested in the shade as the children swam. Her face was weary with motherhood and a collapsed marriage, though the lines had somehow managed to confine themselves to the corners of her eyes and below the mouth. She was thinking about Alan, her ex-husband. It was her fault as well as his that the split had come and she wished she had not been left so full of spite and bitterness. It ruined her for other men. Men like Paul who, she almost believed, genuinely loved her. Even Paul's love made her afraid. He had once said, "I don't think I've ever seen you laugh." If he loved her when she was sullen, would he love her happy? She couldn't change and anyway that was the way to lose, not to win someone. It was the inconsistency of her moods that had

31

driven Alan away. Paul loved a moody bitch. That was up to
him. The strong scent of the fig mingled with that of a nearby
carob tree and she rested her head back on one of the
branches, closing her eyes.

Loraine was so involved in her own unhappiness she did not
notice that her charges had rounded the corner of the bay and
were out of her sight.

Richard never failed to be fascinated by the fact that he could
fly without artificial aids. That was what it felt like, drifting on
top of the water and staring down at the bottom of the sea,
some twenty feet below. It was like lying spread-eagled on a
cloud and floating over the world. A cool, silent and crystal
beauty stretched below him. Another planet altogether. Dust-
covered and primal. Let the old man have his bones – *his* world
was here, below the low tide mark.

He was mildly irritated by some brown limbs that intruded
upon his private thoughts, sending white clusters of spume
over his face mask and a fizzing to his ears. He took a deep
breath from the mini-tank curled like a halter around his neck,
and shook a warning fist at Rosemary.

"Don't do that!" he mouthed at her eyes, light blue behind
the face mask. She gave him a swift mock grin and pointed to
the horn of rock where the waves and currents were twisting
together into a rope of white. He knew she was indicating that
the spot was dangerous but he did not see anything to worry
about. He had swum in the same place many times before,
without women along to hinder him. Besides, they were both
strong swimmers. He shook his head and dived.

Snaking to the bottom he picked out a large smooth rock,
grasped it and then stood on the sandy bottom. He knew Rosemary was watching him as he began to walk, or rather bounce
along, like a moonman in low gravity atmosphere. Then he let
the rock go and bobbed to the surface. Rosemary followed.

"How about that?" he said, as they trod water. "First man in
Cyprus to walk subsurface."

"Man?" she replied, after spitting out her breather. "You're a mere *boy*. Men are large creatures with muscles and brains. ..."

She had already forgotten her own worries about their position. They were both well past the point of the horn anyway, and drifting towards the middle of the neighbouring bay to Fig Tree.

Richard ignored these remarks. Replacing his mouthpiece he dived again and swam down to some fronds that were waving in the currents on the sandy bottom. Suddenly he saw it, near an opening in some rocks and the situation excited him. The object in view was a shell, half-buried in the sand and therefore empty. It was about as large as a bowling ball, brown in colour, and ribbed. A tun shell. What was fascinating about the shell was its position by the small black hole. He had been told that octopuses devour the occupants of tun shells and leave the cases outside their front doors.

He swam cautiously towards the hole and, on reaching it, was unhappy to see that it was only inches deep. Just a depression. Richard was not going to catch an octopus after all. It would have been a great move, he thought, had there been one there. *That* would have sorted the men from the girls. Never mind, he had the shell.

As he reached for the object something jerked at the boy's lungs. He paused for a second, puzzled, and took another breath. None came and his lungs constricted painfully in his chest. He pulled even harder on the breathing apparatus and at the same time kicked for the surface. This time his chest seemed to flatten with the effort of the drag for air which was not there to be had. His tank was empty. Like a fool he had not checked it before the swim. His father would have done, but he was out at the site, digging.

Panic. The mouthpiece was spat out and another breath attempted. An intake under the surface floods lungs with water, not oxygen, and Richard was in serious trouble gulping and choking down the fluid. He began to thrash wildly, forcing his body further away from that light green patch above his head. Another swallow, and pain all around. Finally there was a vague mistiness, like white fungus, spreading through his brain, and the disappearing of the blue-green of his surroundings. Blackness flecked with colour.

His scalp began to cause him trouble; a dull aching forced him to lift a limb ballooning with water. He could only raise it a fraction of an inch. Then he spewed warm fluid over his chest. The arm deflated and a voice said, "Oh please Richard, are you all right? Don't play games if you are. It's cruel. *Please, please* wake up."

Play games? he thought. I should like to play games, when my body empties some more of its unwelcome load. The warm liquid spilled out of his lips again and he slowly opened his eyes.

Rosemary was kneeling over his prostrate body, the front of her swimsuit hanging low. He could see one small breast, cone-shaped and tipped with a soft, dark arrowhead which threatened the centre of his chest.

He had never seen a girl's nipple before – at least not accompanied by a breast, and he felt his abdomen tighten.

"Are you all right?" she asked, seeing his eyes open. Her voice was softer and less anxious now that he was obviously conscious.

"I had to pull you out by your hair – does it hurt much?"

He was afraid to speak in case she moved, his eyes still being held fast by that single droplet of dark flesh that wanted to leave the smooth white stalactite from which it hung. If he could reach out and touch it his belly would explode but as sensibility crept through his brain he realized that such an act was swiftly receding from him. The secret places of women and girls were awesome to the youth and soon he would not be able to blame semi-consciousness for the act.

Suddenly he realized he owed the girl his life. He was both grateful and angry at the same time – a turbulent mixture of these two emotions surged through his aching chest. He was angry because she was a female and she had saved *his* life. It was his dream in reverse.

"Thanks. . . ." he stuttered, still spitting seawater. "I . . . thanks anyway." Then another thought crossed his mind.

"You won't tell anyone will you?"

She leaned down, one hand either side of his head. Rosemary was fifteen years old and wise in the ways of fourteen-year-old boys.

"Has it hurt your pride?"

"It's not that," he said honestly. "I . . . I don't want my father to know. If he knew, well, life would be difficult. You understand that, don't you? You know him."

She sat up on his legs.

"Okay," she replied simply. Then she added, "Yes, I know him. He's practically *my* father too, the time he spends with Loraine." She never called her "mother". Not since her father had left, she had once told him.

"Well, you can't blame him . . ." Richard started to say, then began a fit of coughing. He felt like vomiting, and then did, but spat it out like seawater, hoping Rosemary could not tell the difference.

"Are you sure you're all right . . .?"

"Yes, yes," he answered quickly, feeling anything but well. "I'll be okay. How would you like to swallow a gallon of seawater?"

"You're exaggerating," said Rosemary, standing up. "Anyway, don't think I didn't see you looking at me . . . I didn't realize you'd come round."

His face almost burst into flame at this frank statement. How *could* this girl . . .? Another coughing bout hid his embarrassment and gave him an excuse for his colour.

"Of course," she said, kicking at a sand ripple, "I shan't tell anyone about this: you won't want people to know you were saved by a girl." This last part of the sentence he suddenly realized referred to his school-mates and he understood the double meaning in the words. Females were so damned devious. Stim! He had not even thought about telling his friends. Would he have told them? Perhaps.

"I've seen Rosemary McKinnon's cones!"

35

A statement like that would have given him a lot of prestige amongst the boys at school. Especially since it was true. He knew she was watching him and he attempted to look unconcerned.

"You haven't been telling lies have you?" she said in a tight voice. Females? They always thought the worst of someone. Now he was having to defend himself without being in the wrong. Somehow he was *always* on the defensive with Rosemary.

"No . . ." he growled. "Of course not. What do you take me for? I don't . . . well, I don't lie very often. Not about things like that. Anyway," he flared, "I think we'd better forget it." It was weak, after all that had passed between them.

Richard watched the waves for a while, until the giddiness left him, while Rosemary walked slowly along the waterline picking up shells and examining them. A shout came from the point and both their faces registered annoyance.

"Stim! The beast's found us," said Richard, climbing unsteadily to his feet.

Loraine was standing on the ridge between the two beaches, the sunlight behind her. They could clearly see the outline of her body beneath the thin dress, but to Richard she was simply an old woman. Rosemary muttered, "Remember."

He hissed back, "And you!"

They climbed up to meet the anxious Loraine, lizards scattering with abrupt movements as they progressed. Finally they reached her.

"Where have you been? I've been looking everywhere."

"Sorry," said Richard, hoping to take the brunt of the attack, "we drifted round the point by accident. We've been walking back."

Loraine looked from one to the other and Richard wondered if there was something in their expressions that gave rise to suspicion.

"You've been a long time. What've you been doing?"

Rosemary interrupted with a terse, "Don't be silly Loraine,

Richard's just told you. We've been walking. . . . Stim, I could do with a drink." She changed her tone completely, making it clear the subject was finished with. "Is there anything cool in the slider?"

"We'd better all have a nice long drink," said Loraine brightly.

Now why was she saying it like that? thought Richard. She was talking to them as if they were three-year-olds, and she must know they would resent it. Perhaps she thought . . . well, whatever mothers think. There was only one thing worse than a girl — and that was a grown woman. Obviously they became more suspicious of others as they grew older. Which meant that Rosemary stood no chance whatsoever of escaping such a trait — considering the start she had got.

The three of them strode back towards the slider.

3

A carob tree had become the most hated object in Levan's life. It stood between him and his fame as an archaeologist. He eyed it with intense dislike, the twisting hollow trunk and gnarled branches – an ugly tree, the carob – and he hated it for sinking its roots into the sparse soil gripping the exposed rock with its dry, hairy tendrils. Above the pair of them, the tree and Levan, rose the cliff upon which perched the ruins of an old church. Impassively, church and cliff looked down from their cloudbank heights upon the two antagonists with the vacant faces of ringside spectators relaxing during a lull in the history of the world.

Levan had authority to dig holes on any piece of public land in Cyprus. Many private landowners had also given his trowel access to their possessions. However, there was a centuries-old law in Cyprus, strictly adhered to, which stated that though a man might own the land, he did not necessarily own the trees that grew upon it.

Carob trees were normally owned by families. Levan's obstacle, under which he was sure his Kyrenia Man lay, was owned by a particularly obnoxious family head called Kariyos. (Dig up his tree? He must be crazy. It was his livelihood, to collect the carob beans in season. Yes, he owned several hundred trees on Cyprus, but what if every person in the street wanted to dig up his trees? Money? He had enough money already.) Kariyos senior, a Greek Cypriot in his late sixties, was in fact fairly poor, but he was xenophobic. It said much for his character that he and his family still lived in the Turkish side of the island though most Greeks had been driven out. Stubborn, hard eyes glared from the big-boned peasant face that was as stolid and unmoving as the trunks of his carob trees.

This was the one place beneath the rock shelter where he had not dug. What the hell was a tree doing growing in the entrance to a rock shelter anyway? All around the spot he had found fragments of bone, some of them charred. This had to be the fireplace, under the carob, where the rest of the bones were heaped. Now that the laboratories had confirmed the bone fragments as being around 33,000 years old, he wanted some skeletons to put together. Solid evidence of the existence of a group of people. Neanderthals, probably, but he did not care. So long as nobody could say, "It was a one-off find. One man who probably drifted to Cyprus in a small boat. Spent his last days as a hermit."

Kariyos was coming up the track on a donkey. Damn the man, thought Levan. He wiped the sweat from below his hairline as the baldheaded Greek came towards him, muttering and grunting to his beast, his feet almost touching the ground either side of the unfortunate animal.

"What you want by my tree?" shouted the old man in a heavy accent. "Keep away from my tree."

Levan took his hand from the misshapen trunk. The tree seemed to give out more of its thick, stinking odour as the Cypriot approached, almost as if it were greeting the old man.

"Two stinking bastards together," grunted Levan.

"You keep away from my tree," said Kariyos as he reached the rock shelter, his lips curled back above his stained teeth, showing the effort of his ride.

Levan shrugged helplessly. "What the hell are you doing here?" he asked, in a resigned voice. "How can I damage this great hunk of wood? Pull it out like a weed? It's as solid as a house."

"My tree," said Kariyos, falling rather than dismounting from the sullen-looking donkey. Its coat was matted and wet where Kariyos had been sitting.

"Your tree," repeated Levan. "There's hardly anything left of it to worry about." He indicated the lower branches, which had all been chewed back to the bark by goats standing against the trunk on their forelegs to reach the dark green leaves.

"Why don't you let me dig it up?" He tried one more time. "I've told you I'll pay you ten times its worth."

"No deal," Kariyos grunted. "This is *my* tree. I say who digs here and who doesn't."

For once in his life the old man was on top. The two men faced each other, both similar in build: heavy around the shoulders and jaw, thick-limbed.

"You people," sneered Kariyos. "You think you can come here and take what you want. I've seen you all. You know how old I am? I've seen all the changes. The Turks came through here in the seventies with guns. I was here. I am still here. People!" He spat to emphasize his contempt of the human race. "You know the Greeks? We had this land back to the Athenian, Cimon. You see his statue at Lanarca. You see the great places they left. . . ." Cypriot antiquities were relatively recently discovered structures and therefore superior to those in Greece, ravaged during modern invasions. Cypriots still used the amphitheatres at Curium and Salamis.

"Cimon – yes, he was a sensible man," said Levan.

"So am I a sensible man," said Kariyos. "And you will not take my tree – my carob bean tree."

Levan left the old man kebabing lamb beneath the tree, which gave him an idea. That night he and Richard drove to a dingy stone dwelling three miles west of Kyrenia. Levan had a pocketful of notes which, under the light of a dim lamp, was soon transferred to another, grimier, pocket. Kariyos's relations were not above reproach. His cousins, who also had a part-share in the tree, followed their own separate philosophy.

Two nights later the tree was on fire.

A carob tree burns like a fleece dipped in wax. Its oily properties and the peculiarity of the hollow trunk, which forms a roaring furnace, make it an almost impossible job to quench the flame. Three times the fire department came out to douse the inferno and three times the smouldering trunk reached flash point shortly after they had left it. They gave up and left the giant torch to burn itself out. It was a talking point amongst passengers on passing liners afterwards, especially since it illuminated the white ruins of the church during the night, giving the building an unearthly appearance while the flames lasted.

"The burning bush," said Kariyos, when Levan dared to go up to the site to meet him again. "An old trick landgrabbers use. Don't think you thought of it first. Also Moses. He thought it was God, but it was the landgrabbers."

Levan tried to bluff it out. "I don't know what you mean."

Kariyos laughed humourlessly, bunching his woody fists into hammers.

"Yes. You didn't start the fire in my tree – but it does well for you, eh? A black stump of charcoal is not a tree, eh?"

"That's true," said Levan, in a small voice. "I can dig here now."

Some people were following Levan with tools to remove the tree-stump and to begin the excavations in earnest. He had also sent a telex to Professor Leidermann, the man with the Wiederhaus Repeater. Levan's dream was on the point of materializing – provided they found the skeletons.

"Look," he said to the old man. "I'm sorry it's happened this way. You don't know what this means to me. I've just got to find a man . . ."

Kariyos looked puzzled and Levan realized that he had not fully explained to the old man why he wished to remove the tree.

"Under the carob," he said, "should be the remains of men, something like you and me. But older men – people who walked on Cyprus when the world was a youth, covered in green forests and virgin waters. . . ."

Was he laying it on too thick? The old man's eyes had softened a little.

"I don't like people," replied Kariyos, in a quieter tone.

"But these men were like you, Kariyos – hard, weathered men who lived out of doors. Close to the animals, close to the earth. These were *your* people, and they're buried here. . . ."

Kariyos suddenly flared again.

"You want to desecrate a grave? You ghoul!" The words were

in Greek but Levan understood a smattering and he caught the change in mood, certainly.

"I want to find these men to give them a decent home. Their bones are piled in heaps together, desecrated by time and the elements. I want to fit the bones together. . . ."

The old man changed tack with the ease and rapidity of a small sailing craft.

"You pay me."

Levan was taken aback. "Pay you . . .?"

"You pay me now," the dirty calloused palm was out, "for the tree. What you said before — that much will do." He was the businessman now and Levan was left floundering. These damned islanders. You did not know where you were with them.

"I've already . . ." began Levan, but changed his mind. The old man knew what had happened. He wanted this money now because there was no other way to save face. The money did not really matter to either man, Levan knew. It was a symbol, a gesture. He counted out the notes and put them into Kariyos's hand. The Greek Cypriot would not look at him, but before he climbed onto his patient donkey he said, "You look after my old Greek people, you hear me?"

"I'll look after them," said Levan, and then watched as the donkey swayed downhill with its load. Most of the flies followed the departing couple, they being more interesting than the scrubbed pink flesh that remained under the rock shelf.

When Richard arrived at the site with Rosemary the stump was half out of its bed but still clung, like a blackened, tenacious octopus, to the soil that had bred it. Students from Nicosia University were painstakingly removing the coarse roots from their anchors one by one. Levan used the students, not because they were cheap, but because they were careful. Hired labour tended to be heavy-handed and had no affinity with the work. Student hands were loving. And Richard knew his father liked young people around him.

"Stim," said Rosemary. "Things are really floating around here. I think your father's beautiful, don't you?"

A pang of jealousy went through Richard's body.

"No. Why? Should I?"

"Yes. He's so full of . . . enthusiasm. You know what I mean. He's exciting."

Richard kicked a stone. "And I suppose I'm dull and stupid."

She laughed, upsetting him. "Don't be childish, Rick . . . No, I didn't mean that," she added as he turned away, red in the face. "I mean, well, learn to see what people are really like. I'm fonder of you than anyone else. You know that."

At that point in the conversation there was a shout from one of the diggers. The tree was out and they could go down to the depth they required. Spades bit the dull red earth and sweat rolled down forearms to wet the handles and shafts. For several hours they dug, removing huge rocks and finding everything but the vital remains of human bones. Even Richard and Rosemary got carried away with the fever of the promise of discovery. The universal digger is a man who will turn the earth for anything of worth. Old bottles, swords, toothpaste jars, and heavy metal. He will dig anywhere, at the smallest hint of something hidden below. The universal digger is a solitary man; he does not come in bunches such as those which Levan had recruited. But once the spade has cut the face of the land, and a goal lies inside the darkness of the underworld, the fever can grip any man. When the first bone was uncovered, yellow and black, a scream went up and all physical activity was replaced by a hubbub that would have shaken the foundations of Nimrod's tower.

One by one the bones were uncovered while Levan, a headache raging inside his skull as a result of the sun and excitement, swallowed tablets and ran backwards and forwards collecting his hoard. Finally the trench was exhausted of its treasure and Levan had to be persuaded by his ecstatic group of helpers to accompany them to a nearby bar for a celebration. He was eager to be at work on the find, fitting the charred bones together – almost afraid that he had not un-

43

covered all the pieces — but they would not let him. He was going to get drunk, on Keo hock and Filfar, and his jigsaw puzzle could wait until the following day. The children went home to Rosemary's bungalow to tell Loraine the news.

Paul was on the patio of the beach café when Loraine found him and he waved to her to join the crowd. They had pushed two or three tables together and had almost reached the dancing-singing stage. Empty wine bottles littered the table top and greasy plates with small pieces of half-eaten shellfish were piled high on the table-cloth. Some of the students wore wet clothes and their hair was plastered over their faces. There had obviously been horseplay on the water's edge — perhaps even swimming, one way or another. Loraine was tight-lipped. She did not disapprove of celebrations, but joining in the tail-end jollity of a party when one is still cold sober is an unexhilarating prospect.

"Who's this?" shouted a student, as she stood hanging back on the edges of the dim cones of light which the external lamps cast down.

"It's a lady," answered a chubby girl. As she spoke she leaned backwards and in doing so slipped from her chair. While the attention was on the plump student lying on the floor amongst the fishheads and remains of cold potatoes, Levan took the opportunity to slip away and lead Loraine back to the slider.

"Having a good time with the young ladies?" Loraine snapped, hating herself for being so waspish and petty.

"Yes," answered Paul, in a slightly slurred voice. "And the young men."

They walked on in silence. When they reached the slider Loraine turned and said, "I'm sorry, I don't know why I'm being so stupid. Is it very good news? You found what you wanted?"

Paul grinned at her, the boyishness close to the surface of his broad face.

"That and more. Several animal bones. What I want to do

now is reconstruct a scene of their time using the skeletons. Leidermann's arriving tomorrow."

She was puzzled and then realized what he was talking about.

"Oh, the man with the machine – the repeater thing."

"That's it," he replied. "C'mon. Let's go home and get some coffee. My head is about to explode but I couldn't disappoint my students – they worked bloody hard."

His eyes suddenly shone. "I've got to see them, Loraine. I've got the money and I can indulge myself, without hurting Richard's future. Besides, I think the boy would be better off without all the money. You understand. You *must* understand. A man can dig all his life and find nothing worth anything much – a few fossils, a few bones, but nothing of any significance. Maybe he'll die frustrated – maybe not. Perhaps that's all it takes to satisfy some men. But me! I knew I'd find something big, someday. And this is *it*. This is my day and by God I mean to see every corner of it while the sun's still shining for me. ..."

The hardstanding at the side of Nicosia airport was open to the midday sun. Ghostly serpents of heat stood on their tails out on the peritracks, and porters, mechanics and passengers all moved with the lethargy of horror-movie zombies. Levan was grimy and uncomfortable, but still he felt elated. The flight he had come to meet had been on time and the man he had been expecting was just leaving the customs hall and walking towards him.

Professor Leidermann was thin, delicate, slightly effeminate. He had a beard but the hair grew sparsely in places and became crispy at the jowls. He held the long fingers of his right hand before him and Levan gripped them in greeting.

"How do you do, Professor?" Levan was impressed by qualifications and titles. Especially American-bestowed honorifics.

"How do you do? If you don't mind I'll go straight to the seaport. To see if the equipment has arrived?" he added, seeing

Levan's puzzled look. Although Leidermann had flown to Cyprus he had obviously sent the repeater ahead of him by skipcraft. Probably he did not like sea voyages – or had not the time to enjoy them if he did.

Levan said, "I'll take you – in my slider. I'll see you once you have your luggage."

"Fine. That's very kind of you."

A few minutes later Levan was loading the two small cases into the boot of his slider.

"You travel light."

Leidermann smiled. "Not really. I'm expecting my main luggage to be with the equipment – expecting, not banking on it. I have lost more property in transit . . ."

"I know what you mean. Let's hope the repeater's there okay."

"It's a bit heavy for a pocket." Leidermann laughed: a set of fingernails drawn down a pane of glass. Levan winced and began to hope he did not amuse Leidermann too much during their business together.

"Well," continued the professor, his tone becoming brisk. "What are they, these bones of yours? Neanderthals?"

"Cro-Magnon," said Levan. "At least, I prefer to call them Kyrenia men, but they are Cro-Magnon type." He found it difficult to keep the pride out of his voice.

"And you want me to put flesh on their bones . . .?" The two men were now in the slider and pulling out into the stream of traffic, moving towards the edge of Nicosia.

"I hope you can produce a hologram for me."

"I can. It will cost you a lot of money – as you know. I wouldn't be here otherwise. Strange that the two finds should come at once. Still, yours is the more important of the two in my eyes. . . ."

Levan's heart double-jumped.

"Two finds? What do you mean, two?"

The pencil-line eyebrows were raised.

"You mean you hadn't heard? Someone discovered a Neanderthal – on Troodos early this morning."

Troodos was a range of mountains that formed the backbone of Cyprus – the main peak in that range was Olympus but more often than not the 6,000-feet high mountain was referred to as Troodos.

"A Neanderthal?" Levan was dismayed.

"Well, part of one. Rib-cage missing, apparently, but most of the backbone, the left leg, arms and the skull has been found."

Leidermann seemed to become aware of Levan's depression for the first time. They had slowed to a crawl to allow a shepherd to cross their path and Leidermann was looking at Levan's face with concern.

"My dear sir, are you quite . . .?"

"All right. I'm okay. It's just a bit of a shock."

Leidermann tried to make light of the matter.

"You've no need to worry. You're the man with several complete skeletons! God, this other fellow – what's his name, Plancet – must be feeling twice as bad as you. He's a bounty hunter too, you know. . . ."

The sheep moved on, disappearing into their own dust cloud. Levan had the feeling that he had missed a vital point in Leidermann's last sentence.

"A what? Is that what we're known as?" They picked up speed once more.

"Bounty hunters? – of course. You must be new to the game. Is this your first find?"

Levan nodded. "I'm a virgin," he said, anticipating what was sure to be the slang for an amateur archaeologist without an Early Man under his belt.

"Not any more," chuckled Leidermann. "Your virginity went the day you found that piece of jawbone. And believe me, Mr Levan, there aren't many people who experience first penetration with five complete skeletons. . . ."

Levan glanced round at the professor. That was it! The message was sent *before* the first discovery.

"How did you know that I had five? My messages only said *the possibility of one*."

Again, the chuckle.

"You are naïve for a bounty hunter – it was on the news this morning. You're famous, Mr Levan – or hadn't you heard? The students you hired wouldn't make trustworthy pyramid engineers – a little joke. They visiphoned New York, and London too, I imagine, and Paris, and Rome. The island will be swarming with reporters soon. I should find a nice little hidey-hole . . . Oh, and the skeletons? Are they in a safe place?"

"Well – under lock and key."

A smile from Leidermann.

"For a virgin, you haven't done so badly."

Levan drove Leidermann to the seaport at Kyrenia and then asked him if he would mind taking a taxi to the hotel. The professor seemed surprised but said he didn't mind in the least.

From there Levan drove straight to the set of slider garages that served as his workshops. His heart started racing as he climbed out of the slider hatch and he saw that one of the garage doors were open. Then, almost coinciding with Richard's appearance in the doorway, he remembered that Richard and Rosemary had said they would clean down the bones in the way he had taught them.

"Dad? Where've you been. The visiphone's been blasting away all afternoon. I've switched it to 'busy' – just couldn't keep answering all those calls."

"Are the skeletons safe?"

Rosemary had appeared behind Richard's shoulder.

"Of course," Richard replied. "Why shouldn't they be?" His tone implied he was feeling hurt. "Think we'd drop one?"

"No, no. Nothing like that son. It's just that the whole damned world knows of the discovery now and we've got to make sure we keep them well locked up. I think I'll hire a couple of guards."

"Stim! Those phone calls. They were all from people who wanted to talk about our rattlers."

"Our what?"

"Our bones – the skeletons."

"Oh, I see," said Levan. "Well, you and Rosemary go over to Loraine's now. We'll invite ourselves to dinner. I'll join you in about half an hour. Oh, and thanks for the work you put in. Are they all sealed in plastic now?"

"Finished twenty minutes ago," replied Rosemary. "C'mon Rick, let's go and bully Loraine into giving us plankton steaks."

Levan watched the two lithe, brown-limbed bodies disappear down the hill between the split-level gardens of the neighbours. God, I wish I was Richard now, he thought.

He locked the garage doors securely and then went inside the house. It would take some time for the foreign correspondents to get visas but the locals would be round tonight. The visiphone buzzed before he had time to make an outgoing call. It was a Cypriot news agency. He gave them what they wanted, then punched out the code of a local café. A voice answered in Greek, the picture a poor quality.

"Do you speak English?" asked Levan.

"Yes," replied the gritty face. "I speak it very well."

"Good. Well, look, I'm after a man called Kariyos. . . ."

"It's a common name."

"The man I want is the baldheaded old guy that lives in Karavas. He comes to your café, I know. Rides a donkey."

The voice was guarded. "Why do you want him? Who are you?"

"My name is Levan. Can you tell him I need him? – or rather someone he recommends. It's for a job I want doing." Levan gave the address and the wavering image promised to deliver the message.

"Tell him it's about my old Greek people," said Levan, just before he hung up.

With any luck Kariyos would come over that night, after his evening bottle of kokinelli. Or perhaps one or two of his cousins. They were all a tough bunch. Enough to scare anyone away.

Before he left the house Levan telephoned Leidermann. The professor had booked in and was now in the restaurant, replied the desk clerk. Levan left a message to say he would call again later that evening.

The invasion by the media was not as overwhelming as he had anticipated. After four days the clamourings for interviews started to wane and Levan began making refusals. Kariyos had arrived the morning after Levan had visiphoned the café and the old man was more than happy to threaten foreign visitors with the heavy end of a pick handle when they ventured on to Levan's property. Nor did he confine his favourite curses to foreigners only. He shared them equally with Cypriots if they had no business in the area. Kariyos had always enjoyed being a belligerent, offensive man – to be paid for doing what one liked to do best was a happy state of affairs indeed. There were not many people who had the gall to answer back to the white-bristle face embedded with bleary, bilious eyes. Those that did were quickly informed of a previously unrevealed parentage. While Levan was keeping the world at bay Leidermann was assembling his equipment undisturbed on the spot where the bones were found. If Levan wanted hologram cubes of his five people in their actual environment the repeater would need to encircle that particular place.

There was an intriguing puzzle to be pieced together. The bones had been found heaped together but in a certain orderly fashion. Almost as if they had been buried after being broken down into their component parts. Moreover, some of the bones showed signs of being burnt at one time or another. Charring was usually taken to denote cannibalism but Levan was reluctant to accept this theory without corroborative evidence. However, he had to admit that the evidence which might convince others was in the size of the haul and the fact that the skeletons had been sundered before burial. Was it, he wondered, that he did not want the "image" of the people he had found to be marred by a moral indelicacy? Did he want them to conform to social behaviour patterns acceptable to the twentieth century? Certain parts of the world still had strong religious or instinctive beliefs concerning cannibalism. Levan wanted to keep his cavemen pure in thought, word and deed and that was part of the reason for his reluctance to accept the long-pig theory. However, he also found it strange that the bodies had obviously been buried ceremoniously – not just thrown into a hole in the ground but laid out in a symmetrical fashion, as if the bones were revered. It was, of course, possible that they ate their dead while still holding them holy. Still, the ends didn't quite tie and he would wait for fresh evidence before formulating a theory.

Levan was in the living-room of the bungalow, looking out to sea at the skipship and old screw-driven ships, for there were still a few of the latter in service. Mostly cruise ships for people who wanted to get away from the fast pace of the life on land. Limassol still accommodated large liners in its harbour and Famagusta had a pleasure centre, a marina for yachtsmen whose tastes ran to even older pursuits.

It was a soothing, if a time-wasting hobby, watching the boats gliding or floating by, but good for the soul, Levan considered. He was fondling one of the skulls in his hand, protected by its hermetic seal of plastic, as he traced with his eyes the geometric patterns created by the old ships over the ocean's canvas. The piece of jawbone he had found earlier had fitted the mandible of the youth's skull and it was to this chip of bone he owed his discovery.

It was difficult to believe that the orb in his hand once felt and breathed the Kyrenia air, once let the wind whistle through its teeth, once saw the sun rising and setting on a green, young earth. Funny, thought Levan, most people he spoke to imagined prehistoric men as being skulking, desultory creatures shambling in and out of dark holes. Levan considered them bright, alive people full of exuberance. After the fuss had died down over the skeletons he was going to look for paintings. He hoped his community had had its artists as well as its hunters. Cro-Magnon men had had a beautifully simple style which caught in your throat. A live art. A live people, soon.

4

Like segments of a quartered silver orange the Wiederhaus Repeater stood poised on its points and aided in its balance by its connecting rods, upon the place the carob tree had once defended against Levan. By the trenches, last year's children of that stalwart ogre were throwing out their own stiff leaves. Perhaps one of them would replace its parent? Possibly to meet the same fate one day. Carob trees are fire-prone characters.

Richard had arranged garden seats for the visitors, who sat around the machine in a wide semicircle. Selected members of the news media were present but the places of honour went to Rosemary, Loraine and Kariyos. Levan believed in looking after his own, even if, like Loraine, his own did not seem particularly grateful for the honour. Kariyos was unused to silent, orderly meetings such as this one – they reminded him of the funerals of friendless people where none of the women felt close enough to the deceased to bewail his departing. All other meetings either canopied the area with music and singing, or constituted political arenas for the loudest voices. It was uncomfortable, quietude like this.

Levan was moving around the group satisfying his guests with small snippets of information.

Leidermann, the American professor, was inside the glinting network of rods, arranging the limbs of the skeletons so that the hologram cameras would take their initial three-dimensional cube-shots with the group of Paleolithic people in a tight cluster. After that the cavemen would move around inside the machine's pillars – ghosts of a former world. It was partly illusion and partly reality. A new wonder of the twentieth century that could gather inside its confines the light waves of a bygone age and arrange them in the patterns they had employed over 30,000 years before.

A thick, black power cable snaked its way up the slopes to bare its black carbon fangs somewhere inside the outermost segment of the repeater. The Cypriot authorities had sanctioned a ten-minute drain of power from the local area. The repeater soaked up power in enormous quantities but Levan was footing the bill.

Students, humbled for once by the presence of working professionals (most of whom formed Leidermann's travelling team), stood behind the seated newspeople and kept their unusual peace. It was a hot day but they all wore clothes of some kind over their torsos.

Finally Leidermann indicated to his team, and to Levan, that all was in order and ready for the one o'clock start. Then he threaded his way between the network of outer rods to take his place beside Levan. Raising his hand for a silence that was already as still as the inside of a mountain, Leidermann embarked on his usual presentation.

"My friends. You are about to witness a piece of history. No – a piece of prehistory. You already know that this machine – this equipment – has either destroyed or confirmed several historical suppositions. It is limited in its uses by the size of the area it can cover – which as you can see is very small. There are only three such repeaters in existence. Although both the Eastern and Western Regional Governments are now engaged in building publicly-owned repeaters, those already in existence were constructed by Professor Wiederhaus from funds he raised amongst his friends." Leidermann slapped one of the segments as if it were an elephant's rump.

"This old lady was his first and the size is not governed, as you might imagine, by cost or materials but by the scientific laws it employs. Perhaps, someday, someone will manage to find a formula which will increase its viewing area and we shall have a stage on which armies can march? Perhaps I shall be inviting you to view Marathon or Issus." Kariyos beamed.

"However, today we are here to see the group of men and

women who spawned our race of modern people. They were the fathers and mothers of the only surviving species of Man. Perhaps we have other types – a sprinkling – within ourselves? Who knows. Neanderthal features are evident in many Mediterranean ... but I'm lecturing. It's nearly one o'clock – the magic hour. And I can see you're getting restless. Nothing startling will result from today's viewing, of that I'm certain. We shall see a group of simple, though cultured people (for they had an art which belied their life style) in a situation *that they themselves created in their time*."

With these words Leidermann threw the control switch to the repeater. For a split second nothing happened. The skeletons remained a collection of labelled plasticated bones. Then, as the watchers' eyes began flicking in other directions, to determine whether or not something had gone wrong, a ripple like a heat wave ran through the air inside the segments of the repeater and excitement began to grip the hearts of the witnesses.

Loraine McKinnon was rigid with fear as she watched the flesh gathering upon the bones of the figures within the repeater. The skin of her own face felt clammy as she wiped her brow, and her breath burned in her nostrils.

God! God! What's happening? she thought. Was it supposed to be like this? She would never have attended had she known these horrible creatures with their ugly red bodies would form out of air just a few feet from her. Why wasn't Paul near her to protect her? She wanted to run away but the sight of raw humanity was enervating her mental reserves.

"Stim!" said Richard, almost in her ear.

She watched, fascination mingling with her terror as the ground inside the segments changed. Thick, waxy-leaved plants grew around the prone bodies of the five troglodytes, animal skins appeared upon their torsos and stones were visibly forming out of the dust. It appeared cool inside the segments and this impression tended to calm her. It added unreality to the scene within the machine and reinforced her position in the outside world. Nothing could cross the line between the past and the future. Paul had assured her of that.

One of the Paleolithic people stirred.

Fear came rushing back into her body. She shuddered, unable to take her eyes from the creature. It was a male, that much was plain, with thick, muscled limbs covered in a fine, downy hair. He sat up, blinking blue eyes into the sunlight, a grunt escaping his lips.

She heard it! Why should she hear it if it wasn't real?

Slowly the others rose in a similar manner. Two more men, a youth and a woman. The only evidence of the latter's womanhood was her heavy, drooping breasts. In all other aspects she was like the men. What if one of the men and the woman. . . .? God, no! After all they *were* uninhibited, weren't they? And they didn't *know* they had an audience. Why was she thinking such stupid thoughts? She shuddered and Richard turned and looked at her intently, then back at the arena again.

One of the men stood up and stretched his limbs. He yawned and Loraine saw that several of his teeth were missing on the left side of his mouth and a scar ran from his eye into his beard. He was handsome in an ugly sort of way, she thought. Or was that silly?

The man reached down and picked up a half-eaten root vegetable from the ground and began munching on it. Again, she heard the sounds. The boy was also on his feet by this time, moving around the circle periphery. The nearer he came to the rods which caged him the less distinct became his profile: it furred at the edges and his features grew fuzzy. Nothing could hide the strength in those limbs though. They glowed with physical human power and Loraine shivered again, though not with fear this time.

The youth stooped and picked up a stone. Was it a stone? As he moved back to the centre of the arena she saw that it was a knife-like flint. He offered it to the man who took it and cut a slice of the root away, giving it to the boy.

The woman was still sitting on the ground, looking around her in a bewildered fashion. Then she promptly pushed a finger up one of her nostrils with an exploratory movement. The woman wiped the finger in the dust and then began inspecting her feet. Loraine giggled, making Rosemary look at her sharply. She could not help it though. She had the sudden irrational thought that the cavewoman was about to force a toe where the finger had probed.

"Quiet Loraine," whispered Rosemary. "You're disturbing the others."

Loraine almost shouted at her. How could the child take this experience so calmly? But new generations, she remembered, take for granted what their parents consider awesome. Was she becoming so old that the world was becoming unacceptable?

The other two males were on their haunches, doing something with their flint tools. She looked across at Paul. His enraptured expression told her all she wanted to know. At least *he* was getting his money's worth. She realized also that the cameras would be filming all this and that the resultant hologram cubes would be worth a fortune in themselves. Leidermann and Paul had agreed to share the revenue from that particular spin-off.

Leidermann? She found his face too. It was just as exciting, watching the watchers, and less dangerous to her nervous system. (Every time one of those long-haired red men moved in the arena it made her heart race.) Leidermann was just as enthralled by the spectacle he had helped to produce.

The arena inevitably pulled her eyes back again. God, how long is ten minutes? Suddenly every nerve in her body was taut and her breath came out in a rush of choking fear.

The bright eyes of the boy were only inches away from her own. A ruddy hand of mist was reaching through the rods for her face and someone (Paul?) shouted something unintelligible to her from the other side of the machine. All she heard was her name and then she blotted out the remainder of the words with her screams. Rosemary, unbalanced, fell sideways from her chair and at the same time Richard reached out to ward off the offending limb.

The instant his hand touched the spectral fist there was a flash and both youths stood fused to one another, locked together at the gates of time. Then the power died, the caveboy collapsed in a heap of bones, and Richard was flung violently backwards. He jumped immediately to his feet and began running down towards the sea.

Wide-blue. Deep. Ocean deep. Silence. Enter the silence. Must slide into the quiet of the waters. Stop the head-noise. The blue sea pulling: the hook waves clawing to reach him. Get in, inside, away from the strident noise in his head. Rocks cutting knees, stripping the skin from hands. Never mind, never ... Someone coming, close behind. Into the water, quickly, quickly. The head-sounds. The silence. The cool sea. The deep.

Levan caught up with the youth. They were both waist-deep in the water.

"Richard, stop," cried Levan, his chest heaving with the effort of the run. He was gulping air, trying to find his strength.

It was obvious that Richard had no intention of obeying. He viciously peeled Levan's fingers away from his body. He was as slippery as a green wet rock and Levan frantically clutched at him again. They struggled in the breakers, Richard screaming, desperate to put an end to the tumult in his mind, Levan sobbing for breath and swallowing water as his son pulled him down into the foam. Levan had not known that the boy was so strong. With a last mighty heave the man managed to make the boy lose his footing and they both took the impact of the next wave in the chest. Unbalanced, they were bundled together into the shallows.

With all sense of propriety gone, in what Levan now realized was a fight to save his son's life, he grabbed Richard by the hair and dragged him from the water. Then he bent down to get a better grip of the youth under his armpits. Richard twisted and bit him savagely on the chin.

"That's it!" said Levan, and, partly out of pain-induced anger, partly out of necessity, he hit Richard under the chin with a blow that would have felled a man.

"You'd better get some tetanus shots when you go down to the hospital," said Loraine.

They were on the balcony of Levan's bungalow. Levan himself was in a mild state of shock. Loraine had been cleaning the crooked wound made by Richard's teeth.

"My son is dirty?" said Levan.

Loraine replied, "That's not what I mean and you know it. Just get the jabs and don't argue." She was a good woman to have in a crisis. No nonsense. She might not laugh very often, thought Levan, but she rarely cried either.

"Poor Richard," said Levan for the third time. "I didn't mean to hit him as hard as that."

The blow had badly bruised the youth's jaw. At first Loraine had been afraid that Paul would blame her for the accident — it was because of her that Richard had reached out and touched the rods of the Wiederhaus Repeater. At least that was what Leidermann considered responsible for the flash. He said it could not have been the caveboy's hand because there was no hand to touch. It was not a solid entity. It was the American's guess that some of the power had shorted into the framework. With such enormous current flowing into the machine Richard did not even need to physically touch the metal — the power could jump the space, like a spark jumped across the gap in a plug from an old-fashioned combustion engine.

"He was lucky not to have been killed," Leidermann had said. Then, rather tactlessly, he added, "Of course, there may be brain damage."

Levan had replied, "In which case I'll sue you for everything you've got. Why didn't you warn us that the machine could be dangerous?"

"It isn't dangerous," Leidermann insisted, "Not unless someone interferes with it."

"That still makes you responsible."

Leidermann refrained from replying. It was useless to argue with a man as emotionally disturbed as Levan was at present. He *had* warned the man of the potential danger of the machine – in fact it was in their contract. The repeater was a new concept in electro-physiology. It was bound to have unknown and, indeed, unforseeable side-effects. What man in Levan's position – a man who has just hit the supreme heights in his field – listens to or reads warnings which might spoil the fruits of his success?

They had parted company without another word spoken between them. Leidermann had an appointment with the Neanderthal Man on Mount Olympus. Levan had gone home with Loraine.

Later that evening Levan visited Richard in Akrotiri hospital. He was still unconscious but not from the blow on the jaw. The doctors had drugged the boy to relieve him of the pain he complained was in his head. Sitting by the boy's bed in the darkened room Levan stared moodily out of the window at the bouncing sea below. Akrotiri was a military base situated on a cape – Levan had chosen to have Richard taken there by skip-boat because in his view it had the finest doctors on the island.

He was willing to admit that he only considered it so because some of his own countrymen practised there. A man turns to what he *knows* in an emergency. The unknown may equal or better the treatment but, if he can get it, a man will usually choose what will lay comfortably on his mind, unpricked by doubt.

Levan sat by his son for almost two hours. All the pleasure of the discovery, and of indulging in the subsequent Wiederhaus Repeater show, had been negated by the incident that coincided with the termination of the performance. It was a high price to pay for success – a fourteen-year-old son with possible brain damage. Levan had always partly believed in the maxim that you always pay for good fortune, one way or another. This was a cruel exchange.

He returned to the hospital the next morning. Loraine had

been waiting for him when he arrived back that evening but he had been in no mood to salve her conscience. A few words from him might have eased the guilt she felt at her part in the affair — if she had not screamed — if she had been watching all the time instead of being more concerned with the onlookers — if so many things. He had not been prepared for her reception, however, the self-recriminations, the abject words, and he had been hard on her, telling her shortly that she had better go to bed — in her own bungalow — and leave him to his thoughts.

Pulling her poncho over her head she had left without another word. He had been sorry after she had gone and considered calling her back to apologize but finally let the night slide on, falling asleep in a wicker garden chair on the balcony.

On waking he had not only felt stiff but heavy: an all-over heaviness as if his blood had been syphoned off during the night and replaced by mercury. It had weighed him down and he trudged around the house forcing himself to eat a sandwich. *Weltschmerz*, he thought to himself, trying to lighten his load.

At the hospital worse news was awaiting him. Richard was awake but seemingly unaware.

"Unaware of what?" asked Levan of the young doctor that had been present when he entered the room.

"Well, er, unaware of anything. He just can't be roused."

Levan took a quick look at Richard who was propped up in the bed. The room was no longer gloomy now the sunlight streamed onto the white walls. It was so bright it seemed that nothing bad could contaminate such a sparkling atmosphere.

"His eyes are open," said Levan. "What do you mean by 'roused'?"

The doctor coughed. He said, "Unfortunately we opened them. That is to say that we had to physically open the lids."

"And then what?"

"Nothing, nothing at all. He won't speak or acknowledge our presence in any way. He'll ... perform his functions, though not to order. . . ."

"He did it in his bed?" said Levan in an incredulous tone.

"He can't help it, Mr Levan. We have to force-feed him,

60

almost. That is, he'll swallow if we're patient with him – which of course we are," he added hastily.

Finally Levan said, "I suppose it's a coma or something. You do *know* what it is?"

"Not exactly."

"What does 'not exactly' mean?"

"It means," replied the younger man, "that we aren't sure. We've never seen anyone behave quite like Richard before. His brain is working. I mean, he feels pain and he can move parts of his body, but the movements don't seem to co-ordinate: they're only reflex actions. They are not responses that originate from mental understanding. They don't result from *reasoning* – there's no thought process. . . ." The doctor drew in a deep breath. "In other words, the brain is alive but the mind has gone. It's not producing anything."

"This is terrible" said Levan in a broken voice. He sat down in a chair proffered by the doctor and stared at his son. He was an imaginative man and many times during his life he had, in the middle of night, conjured disasters from minor incidents – tortured himself to sleep with thoughts of the worst. Always, before now, he had awoken to a reality which destroyed the nightmares with a single blade of bright daylight. This time the bad dream was the reality – it had not followed the night back into its daytime retreats in caves and holes in the ground.

"I want to get him to a specialist," he finally said to the young man beside the chair.

"I *am* a specialist." The reply was firm and confident. "Besides, I would not advise moving him just yet. It's possible the condition may go as quickly as it has come. I can find no physical damage."

Levan was hardly listening.

"I want a good man – the best. Name me the best and where I can find him. I have plenty of money. . . ."

"Mr Levan."

This time Levan looked up into the young doctor's face and saw a determined expression.

"What?"

"I *am* the best. Oh, I know what you're going to say – I'm too young, how could I have had the experience . . .?" He paused. "I have not always been the best neurologist in this part of the world, Mr Levan, but recently my father died. I am now . . ."

"This part of the world?"

"Go to America – take the risk of the flight – you'll find one to equal me. You won't find a better man, just one as good. My father was *the* best, and I say that without bias. He was acknowledged so, even by his rivals. He trained several others – myself being one. I'm not all that young, Mr Levan – I'm thirty-one. You don't have to be old to be good."

Levan appraised the doctor again and after a long, searching look asked, "Are you an American?" The doctor's accent was stateside.

"Dutch."

"Well," said Levan, "I don't suppose nationality has got much to do with anything. I'll leave him in your hands." He stumbled out of the chair and towards the door.

"Please give me a call when there's any change. I'll leave my number with the receptionist . . . no, she already has it. I'll just . . . go and get some breakfast," he finished helplessly.

He drove his slider through the shallows of Salt Lake, scattering the flocks of flamingos into clouds of pink talcum, and headed through the orange groves towards Episkopi. He would take a room there until the boy was either better or ready to be moved. As he neared the crossroads he saw the warning lights before the monorail track flashing alternately yellow and red. That would be the midday Ktima–Famagusta express, he thought.

The express duly sizzled through at supersnake speed and Levan took the slider up and over the ramp which connected with the Episkopi road. The old strip of tarmac climbed uphill and wound along the edges of the earthquake-scarred cliffs. On the way it offered the antiquities of Curium Amphitheatre and the Temple of Apollo. Levan, for once, was uninterested in the whiteness of their stones.

Finding himself a hotel room was difficult. It was the tourist season. Eventually a backstreet shop-owner however offered him the room above his dingy trading premises. Levan accepted, then went to a public visiphone booth without bothering to look at the flat. He would only be sleeping there anyway. In the booth he punched Loraine's code. Rosemary's red hair and freckled face came into view.

"Where's your mother, Rosie?" he asked.

"She's in the shower, and I don't like Rosie any more than Loraine likes Lorrie," she answered. "I'll get her for you."

"Precocious brat," muttered Levan, annoyed.

A little time later Loraine appeared, her head wrapped in a towel.

"I'll be staying at Episkopi for a while," he said abruptly. "Keep an eye on Kariyos for me. Tell him to use the house while he's looking after the skeletons."

"I . . . oh, all right. When will you be back?"

"Richard is . . . he's extremely ill. He can't be moved. . . ." There was a sound in the background and Levan realized that Rosemary could hear. He had to tell Loraine, though. There was an obstruction in his throat.

"He's lost his memory – in fact he doesn't even remember me. He just stares, vacantly . . . my God, Loraine!" He found he was weeping and she said she would be right over. That, in itself, would have been the balm he needed, but she added, "Alan's on his way here, to Cyprus. He's a good man in a crisis . . . !"

Then she hung up, leaving Levan distraught and wondering what the hell kind of woman throws an ex-husband at her lover when he's floundering in the quicksand of a nightmare.

Alan McKinnon was tall, broad-shouldered, narrow-faced. He was the type of man you would expect to see playing a sport during his leisure hours – but not a body-contact game like football or boxing. He was too smoothly groomed for that. He was in fact a ski champion and played good club tennis. His skin was dark and tanned easily: he enhanced it with down-white shirts. The blue eyes looked as if they could cut glass and had just that touch of the devil-crazy in them to attract the type of woman that likes to burn her fingers.

McKinnon crossed the Toronto airport lounge and spoke softly to the Air Canada girl. She smiled.

"Your ticket please, sir?"

"Alan McKinnon," he said. "Travelling alone." The last word was heavily emphasized.

"I don't go with the flight, Mr McKinnon," she replied. "I stay on the ground."

"I bet the hell you don't," he said. "I'll be coming back, so don't run away," he flirted.

"What about my boyfriend?" she said.

"Oh, I don't mind if he runs away."

The banter over, he made his way through to the hand-luggage check. The girl had been pretty, he thought. But then he had had a few of those. He liked to analyse his attitude towards females and sex. It helped to pass the time. He loved his ex-wife, for instance, and he had loved the young girl for whom he had left her. In fact, he loved all the women who had entered his life. If you asked each one of those luckless females (bar the eighteen-year-old banker's daughter he had left mussing the bed that morning) they would probably say Alan McKinnon would not know the meaning of love if he read every definitive work on the subject that had ever been written. McKinnon, however, always asked for the definition of love — the true and unequivocal definition — when challenged by his erstwhile bedfellows. Only Loraine had managed to parry that one successfully.

"If you need to define it, you're more shallow than I gave you credit for Alan," she had said on their parting.

Well, he was going back to her now. That was something he had never done with any other woman. Once the bed went stale on him he had always looked for fresh sheets. He was willing to admit that he had another motive, but he was, he told himself, quite looking forward to seeing his redhead again.

And then there was Rosemary. Time he saw his kid again. She had to be a looker if she took after her mother – and him.

A shadow passed in front of McKinnon as he walked down the interconnecting corridor. He glanced nervously over his shoulder and saw a tall farmer-type wearing a broad-brimmed hat. Not the sort at all. Anyway, they wouldn't be interested yet. He had, he thought, at least two months' grace. Then he could begin to worry.

His thoughts ran on again. Yes, the trouble with screwing was the instant the last shudder of the climax had left his body, it was as if he had never had the girl at all. Some people, he knew, experienced a sort of afterglow of satisfaction. He had never felt that. It was useless for McKinnon to argue that his women numbered in hundreds and had been all the colours of the human race. He just did not *feel* anything when he tried to recall the details. It was, he repeated to himself, as if they had never happened. They were history. That was his trouble, why he could not stay away from the young ones. They always knew something different.

He allowed his bag to be passed through the viewer and walked through the frame at the side. Terrorism – hijacking aircraft – was no longer the prerogative of fanatics, as it had been twenty years earlier. It was now a sport. In the early nineties the oil had all but dried up. Gobbled in gallons by the war and greedy New World, the undersea discoveries had soon disappeared. Following the war (which, not surprisingly, was fought with conventional weapons in sporadic bursts over widely spaced areas – the media labelled it the "Fragmented War") the newly formed United World instituted a research programme to find a new fuel. After five years of application the best brains humanity could muster in the field came up with the energy brick – a solid "battery" charged in oceothermal power stations. It was light in weight and the manufacturing process was cheap to establish, both in plant and materials. The brick was developed from a compound known as SAM (an anagram of the initials of the project's head scientist). SAM was a substance with the abnormally high number of 300 allotropes, whose transition temperatures, at normal atmospheric pressure, were closely spaced. It did of course revolutionize transport almost overnight.

Recently, however, the kids – the young people – had been listening to a lot of old tapes produced by forgotten names who had once fought for forgotten causes. Young people try to emulate their old-world peers. They attempt to identify with heroes and heroines of another age. They consider their present life boring in the extreme. So hijacking airliners had once again become a headache for the authorities, only this time there were no demands for the release of political prisoners, or a million dollars cash, or the supply of arms to Bagatoria, or even Freedom for an oppressed nation that was quite happily chugging along and had no interest in, nor previous knowledge of, the Bagatorian Freedom Fighters. This time it was demands to be flown low over the North Pole to watch the oldies squirm in their seats and for the prestige it gave the hijackers on return to home – amongst their "peers" of course. There was even a North Pole club for Teenagers who had "made" the trip.

McKinnon took a seat in the inner lounge and browsed through some of the available magazines. Occasionally he was distracted by a female. Occasionally his guts were "gripped", as he called it, for no apparent reason when a male accompanied the female. He weighed the potential of all men against his own known prowess and was only satisfied if left in no doubt that he could "take" the other man if necessary. The muscles in his abdomen would then relax their tightness. McKinnon had defined the limits of his metaphorical "territory" while still at school and he knew just how far he should allow the other man to go. There were no mistakes allowable. Violence was not only the answer, it was the question also. If a man insulted him by word or gesture, that man paid.

Eventually his flight number was called and he rose with the casual ease of a lion about to enjoy a stroll after a day of lazing under the sun. He crossed the thick red carpet to the flight tunnel, his expensive shoes leaving dents in his wake that gradually disappeared like footprints on seawashed sand. Just as he was about to pass the stewardess at the entrance to the tunnel something touched him on the shoulder, as lightly as the brush of a falling leaf. He felt it and froze. The shadow of the tall, wide-brimmed hat formed a distorted black-mountain shape on the white tunnel wall to his right. He looked up into the face and found the eyes staring knowingly into his own.

Don't forget to come back to us McKinnon, said the expression, without betraying any trace of sinister intent.

McKinnon's guts turned from rock to water in moments, and only when he finally entered the tunnel did he begin to relax again.

5

Suddenly, Richard could see.

The light was dim and grey, like those winter dawns he had
known when visiting England. A musty smell accompanied the
light, seemed to be part of it, and he was aware of a stone
ceiling which opened out a few yards later to an overcast sky. If
this was *death* it was a very normal-looking place to which it
had taken him. It appeared to be a cave — or something like a
cave. His head turned to the left of its own will and he perceived a creature with a man's body and a stag's head and
antlers near him. It was sitting crosslegged, regarding him intently. Was this some mythical heaven to which he had been
wafted? How many different heavens were there? Strange, that
he could contemplate his fate with such detachment now that
he had found the use of his sight. But inside the head he felt
secure — protected.

"Arau crala Esk," said the stag's head.

His own mouth answered in similar gibberish and the stagman leapt to his feet and began dancing, raising dust. People
came running then; normal people with normal heads — and
they began shouting and pointing at him. They wore animal
skins and had long hair. Their bodies were tall and muscled.

"Arau crala Esk," they shouted.

Their arms were like the knotted branches of smooth-limbed
trees and their legs quick to move. Their voices were deep and
welcoming and he knew they were pleased to see him.

Him? Richard?

No, they were seeing the other boy, the one beside him in
the head. This was his companion's body and Richard was a
guest. A visitor in another boy's skull.

The head moved to the right and his face smiled at an old

woman, crouching some yards away. She nodded seriously and the companion said something with the mouth. The woman nodded again. Richard saw that her breasts were bare. Large, bucket-like mammaries hung from her chest but he felt no embarrassment. It was as if he himself was hidden behind a door, looking through the cracks in the woodwork. Only his companion knew he was present and there was a certain disbelief attached even to that knowledge.

The eyes went back to the stagman. Was this a fantasy world? thought Richard. Had he passed through the walls of his own mind into the dream-world at the back of his brain? Halfmen, half-beasts? They existed only in the realms of the mad or . . . or in the ancient world. He studied the body of the manbeast and realized where he had seen it before, that rusty skin — it belonged to one of the Paleolithic men from the arena. . . .

The Shaman removed his headdress and nodded gravely at Esk.

"The Mother has returned you. You must thank Her for Her kindness." The boy was weak from lack of food, but he replied quickly. "I shall, I shall. How long have I lain here? I felt the burning of the fire-eye's spear when the high, black mists would not let his shining through. It touched my inside head."

His mother, the crouching old woman, answered him.

"For two turns of the fire-eye. We feared you were dead. Did you travel far? Into another place?" (Hopefully. Esk was to be special.)

Esk tried to remember his dreams. He wanted to tell them all how he felt but was a little afraid. Only the Shaman, Granla, was allowed to talk magic and speak of other worlds. Esk decided to risk his life. It was his one opportunity to meet fame halfway, and what boy can resist that, even at the risk of death. Death was no great thing to a Gren youth anyway. It happened every day.

"I went a long way into the world of ice-eye and have returned with a companion. He is here, in my head, beside me."

The crowd drew back, a murmuring on their lips. All looked to Granla for his reaction. Granla was old, all-knowing, and he

69

was the warrior chieftain as well as the religious leader. His word was law.

(The Shaman considered the boy's words quickly. Esk was frightened, he could see that. Would the youth lie and put his life at risk purely to enjoy being a celebrity for a brief period of time? He doubted it. Therefore at least an element of truth lay behind the words. The Shaman had been looking for a successor for some time and Esk was one of his favourites. . . .)

"Let the boy rest," he said. "He has been on a long journey."

Thereafter Esk began to enjoy a certain amount of petting from the females, and acknowledgement from the males. He did realize, though, that any rise in status would depend upon his body developing into a stronger, harder unit than it was at that time.

Esk was also wise enough to see the political motives behind Granla's inference that Esk would graduate to leadership. Granla was by no means in his dotage but his body must weaken some time. By pointing towards Esk he would take the attention away from himself – the young, wild youths would turn their jealous eyes towards the successor. At very least it would split the forces ranged against the Shaman.

The caveboy was given some food – strips of fat-slimed meat – to inject some energy into his body. After two days without sustenance his body was weak and listless. Richard found himself wanting to taste the food on the tongue of the caveboy but quickly withdrew from the strange flavour. He had eaten "real" meat many times before but nothing as strong-tasting as half-cooked venison. He did not find it unpalatable – just odd.

Afterwards there was water in small amounts.

Once he had rested, following the meal, Esk began to look around him. There would be some jealousy amongst his contemporaries now that Granla had let fall the innuendo concerning Esk's possible inheritance.

Even now Reng was snarling in his direction, thought Esk. He knew he would have to fight his older half-brother soon. He was not looking forward to that. Reng also had a following among the other youths of the group. It was in the balance whether they would move against Esk, even if he won. Each day he managed to avoid the confrontation was to his advantage. He needed growth and strength.

Reng came over to where he sat.

"I see only one head," he said. "Where is this second person?" Arms folded, legs apart, he waited for an answer.

Their mother, Lelka, tried to intervene.

"Leave the boy alone, he's ill – can't you see?"

"Be quiet, woman," answered Reng, not taking his eyes from Esk. "I asked the *boy*." He emphasized the last word.

"You want to fight me Reng? But not now. When you do, you will need to bring your magic . . . ha, you have no magic," Esk added as he saw the flush rising to his half-brother's face.

"But I have the webs of ice-eye in my mind," Esk continued. "I can spin with my new companion a net to hold Reng fast while my spear finds his heart."

Reng recovered his composure.

"You speak in riddles. When the time comes I will destroy you quickly enough."

Then he strode away to rejoin his gang who waited for his return before throwing insults over their shoulders at Esk and his mother. The old woman took little notice. She was used to the taunts of the youths.

"Have you really taken some magic, like the Shaman has, Esk?" she asked him in an awed voice. "The Shaman danced over you in his animal form for a turn each of the fire-eye and the ice-eye. Some of his own magic must have passed into you."

Esk said, "I have my own – I do not need that which the Shaman has."

Then he stood up and walked down the hill towards the shore. The gasp behind him came from Lelka as he knew that what he had just said almost amounted to heresy. Everyone needed the Shaman. From Granla came all things for he was from the womb of the Earth-Mother Herself. A Shaman is born in the guise of a human, from a woman, but he is placed inside the womb during darkness by the Mother herself, transferring Her unborn child to the mortal woman's passage, using the form of a rampant stag. It was a strange conception, the Mother manifested in the shape of a male beast impregnating a mortal female with the seed of Her child. When Esk became Shaman, his mother would suddenly recall the act with the vividness of a hunter's moon.

Lelka would also become a celebrity should her son be made Shaman.

Esk walked to the very touch of the waves and stared into the water. He disliked the sea. It was full of monsters with knife-sharp jaws and if you went too far out the water stole the breath from your chest and pulled you underneath. Down there were the Agrils — dwarves who cut your body into small pieces and used the meat to trap the game of the sea: knife-fish.

The water looks good. He felt the thought and rejected it. Then it came again, bouncing back, not in words, but there just the same.

The water is good. Deep. Silent. Comforting.

No, he replied. The sea is bad. Full of bad dwarves and killer fish.

Good.

What was this? His companion? The Other? He could feel him, in his head, restless to enter the waves that snatched at his feet. Was the Other mad? Surely he must know, being magic, that the sea held death in every curl on its green-hoary head?

Other, he said in his mind, go back to sleep. This is my body. I tell it what to do. Find your own body if you want to walk to your death.

I move like a fish in the sea.

Not in my body, you do not, replied Esk firmly. The only things belonging to me which go into the sea are my bone hooks or my harpoons.

You are a fool. I know all about the sea.

Revolution! Mutiny!

Esk had had enough of his companion. It was time the Other was taught his place. He tried pushing him to the back of his mind and forgetting his presence there.

72

It worked for a time. Then the Other came back again, resolutely.

(The body belonged to two of them now, and Esk would be taught that he could not monopolize the thought patterns running through his brain. The control of the physical functions of his body would not always remain with Esk. He had to share not only his intellect but his whole being.)

Richard stared at the world around him after having forced his way to the fore. The caveboy was exhausted, had fallen asleep and was therefore no longer able to hold his position of dominance. When he was awake, he was the strongest – possibly because it was, after all, his time, his place. Inherently his, intrinsically his.

It had been a deep evening, and the sky had run with the redness of the meat they had eaten earlier. Now the darkness had settled like coal dust upon the trees and rocks.

In this strange place in which Richard found himself trapped, there were still some things that remained the same, even before the passing of 33,000 years. Some of the components which made the world were immutable.

The sky held the same colours – and the moon's purple features still patched its gold. The sea, too, was the same, with the reflections of the stars running over its ripples like silver creatures boating on a pond. The shoreline was different, of course, and the land and forests frightened him with their wildness. Danger was commonplace in this time. And the climate was colder, much colder, than in the Cyprus of Richard's era.

"Who is walking?" growled someone in a voice laden with sleep. Then silence again, except for the gentle sounds of snoring and the animals scuffling in the world that ringed the rock shelf.

Richard had not understood the words but he guessed they were intended for him. When the caveboy was awake a diluted translation came through to him in the form of jumbled thoughts. When someone spoke Richard understood the meaning, rather than the words. Esk was still asleep, mentally exhausted by his activities during the day.

They had climbed to the top of the cliffs and built a channel of logs along which the men would drive the wild deer tomorrow. Richard had not seen a tame deer, let alone a wild one. It would be exciting to watch the trap being used. Esk had many names for the deer according to their age, sex and shade, and he had thoroughly confused Richard as his mind wandered over their differences in random order. Esk had names for the stars, too, and a word for each wind that touched his skin: he classified them by their strength, direction and temperature. Richard had landed in a time when the Earth and the life that crawled upon it were almost one, almost a part of each other. The wind, the rock and the lizard were bound as tightly to Esk as the coloured threads forming a pattern in an American Indian's blanket. They were just as meaningful to each other, and to the whole, as those patterns. They spelled out existence. Esk knew the lizards as well as he knew his own fingers – the beetles and bugs like his own toes.

Richard could not tell one frog from another, if they were of the same species, and would have laughed if you questioned him about their smell. Esk could tell you the differences between two twin amphibians and could smell how many were hidden in the grasses within a radius of five feet.

The instincts of the animals belong to Man. In Esk's time men were superior to animals because they had all the latter's attributes plus the power of thought.

In Richard's time it was only Man's devices that maintained his superior position over the creatures of the wild.

Before the evening had moved into night Richard had watched Esk making some blade tools out of a block of flint. The caveboy had taken the large nodule of flint and squared the ends off by striking it with a wooden rod. Then the boy had taken a piece of strong pointed bone and using it had applied pressure to the edge of the flint block. Each time he did so a narrow parallel-sided blade of flint sprang off, sharp as the edge of a knife – that being its destined purpose. At the end of the exercise the core of the flint was furrowed with grooves around its circumference where the slivers had been pressed out.

Richard knew from his father that this was an advanced form of tool-making. Earlier types of men had merely split flints with other rocks and worked the edges – later still they had made flake tools by striking the flint with a softer substance such as wood or bone. Blade tools belonged, in the main, to Modern Man.

"What am I doing here?" Esk had awoken and had rushed to the fore. The Mother was asleep and Esk was exposed to the evils that wandered abroad during the hours when the mother was not awake to protect him.

"The Lundren!" Esk looked wildly about him, then hurried back to the fire outside rock shelter. He nestled down between two others and lay there, shivering in the cold night air, afraid to look for a blanket to cover himself.

Richard had caught the picture of the Lundren – huge, predacious birds with eyes that burned out of black faces.

Where do these creatures come from? he asked of Esk.

They live under the ice-eye. When the light comes they turn back into the rocks: into the forms from whence they came.

You mean they become stone during the daylight?

Esk showed him pictures of rock; hunched formations that had a resemblance to shapes of birds. Possibly limestone that had been weathered, thought Richard, but more than likely the sculptor had been human. The lines would have been kept deliberately vague. It would give weight to the theory that these supernatural agents of night possessed strong powers of deception. Besides, a barely recognizable form is more sinister than one that displays its lines openly. Hollows hold shadows, form eyes, hooked beaks, talons.

You are a fool. These are make-believe birds.

Almost before the thought was out Richard heard the beating of the giant wings on the air; saw the heavy shapes plummet down upon the helpless child. The infant was borne off, into the darkness, its blood running in a thin line above the high trees. Flailing arms, thrashing wings, the tearing of claw-held meat.

What was that?

My younger brother, replied Esk.

As the caveboy shivered himself fitfully to sleep again, Richard was left unsure of his disbelief. Could there be some truth in the pictures? He was not in his own time, in his own world. He was in a time older than the coming of witches. Older than wizards. He was out of his depth. His father was more than just a journey away. Reality lay somewhere in the incredibly distant future and Richard began to give way to despair. For the first time he considered his plight in terms of living for the rest of his life in the primitive, savage body of a long-dead boy.

Help me, he whispered in a thin voice, full of the anguish of a lost child — lost in a time when there was not one familiar creature, one feature, one blade of grass that he knew, on the whole face of the earth.

Help me father. Come and fetch me home. Please come.

His one thought was that his father was doing something to rescue him. Richard was too close to adulthood to have faith in desperate hope. Although he knew his father would be as anxious to find him as he was to return he could only guess, blindly, at the situation he had left behind. Perhaps his body had been burned to a crisp and there was nothing to return to? Perhaps they were already weeping over his ashes, at home, 33,000 years away?

The following morning Esk was wakened roughly by Reng and Richard retreated instantly away from the pain to the insulated parts of the brain where touch and smell — the stink of cold fat and excrement — could not reach him. At least he was safe in that respect. As long as he was not to the fore he would suffer no pain nor discomfort. Perhaps, he thought with a philosophical depth he was unused to, he would be the first human able to watch his own death from a distance, cool and detached.

Esk felt the stab of his brother's toe, however, and he snarled at the bullying youth.

"The hunt," said Reng smiling maliciously. "You wouldn't want to miss the hunt, brother."

Esk immediately came alive.

The hunt! Today!

Already the excitement surged through his limbs.

You will like this, my companion, he thought. Are you there? Don't sleep now, for today is the hunt. We have found the deer. We shall eat well tonight. Esk was aware of the Other, sullen in the background and mentally he shrugged. Let him be miserable. The hunt would soon bring him forward.

Esk's mother had tended the fire throughout the night and she hung over it now, her greasy deerskin almost in the flames, one slack breast feeding the infant strapped to her hip with thongs.

"Food, Esk. Have some soup — it's hot and sweet with honey."

The caveboy gulped the liquid greedily from the shell container. There were no pots, no clay containers. Only natural objects served for utensils, and skins for carrying water.

"Nice?" she said, pleased that the boy was filling himself. He needed the strength. The hunt would be arduous. He nodded absently. When he had finished he gave his new sister, the baby, a brush with his hand and then jumped up and went to witness the Shaman calling to the Mother for luck in the hunt.

The Shaman was wearing his face of the stag — the antlers tall and heavy on his head — and therefore *was* the stag. The Mother tossed Her pine top hair in the wind as Her Shaman chanted praises into the morning stillness. She beat Her breast with long, wet arms along the beaches in a display of joy and affection for Her people. She pulled the fire-eye from his bed in the sea to warm away the frost on her belly. It was a sharp, clear morning and the Paleolithic hunters stamped their feet into the red cheeks of the Mother who sang Her pleasure through the grasses on the hill.

When the ceremony was over, Esk collected his hunting spear and carved bone spear-thrower from the armoury at the rear of the shelter. He would need all the magic these objects held if he was to be successful. Humans were not the only animals that hunted deer. The carnivores of the forests would also have their yellow eyes upon the herd that had crossed the mountains.

In the wide belt he had spent so many hours beating and chewing to softness he put his long-handled knife. Richard, whose interest had been thoroughly aroused by the pre-hunt dance and was now intent on missing nothing, wondered why there were no axes or bows and arrows evident. He flashed a picture to Esk.

A bow and arrow?

For making fire? thought Esk. Why should I make fire? The one we have still burns strongly.

No, for hunting!

You can't hunt with such a small spear, replied Esk, dismissing it in contempt. Richard did not follow it up. He deemed Esk unworthy of the effort.

A group of some twenty men and seven or eight boys were waved away from the rock shelter by the women. Esk noticed a very special sign from a young woman, just a little older than he was himself, and felt his abdomen go tight. She was Reng's woman, and a lot of trouble, but reckless thoughts wound through his head. Richard recoiled from these pictures of Esk, sating his appetite between the muscled thighs of the ugly wench with the large sensuous lips, and attempted to push forward to feel the coldness of the morning air. Esk would not let him, however, and as the group climbed higher into the mountains the caveboy's passion was forced into limpness by that increasing coldness. Eventually they reached the place where they had buried sharpened stakes, forming a narrow avenue to the cliff's edge, their points slanting inwards.

Trackers were despatched in all directions to locate the herd while the Shaman and his hunters waited impatiently for the word. Finally it came. The herd was on the slopes in the direction of fire-eye. A pass would need to be blocked and beaters were required to make their way down-wind until they could come up behind the herd. Esk was to be one of the beaters.

Excitement was hot in his nostrils as he moved stealthily beside Reng, all hostility put aside for the event. Such a large herd had not come within striking distance for many a turn of the fire-eye and there would be skins and meat in plenty. Some of the carcasses would be taken into the mountains, above the snowline, to be hung from a cave roof where they would remain frozen and out of reach of large carnivores. Others would be eaten that night. If any animals were crippled, they would be kept alive as long as possible before becoming meat for the eating – survival depended upon keeping the meat fresh and the pain of a crippled deer weighed little against such important issues.

Esk's fine sense of smell could have found out all manner of creatures in the damp grasses but he allowed his senses only one direction – the hunt! His spear, already in the notch of his thrower, felt comfortably heavy in his hand. The point of it glinted with fire-eye's smile. His eyes found details in the plants and rocks that passed beneath his feet.

The air was charged with stone.

Clouds of granite rolled their smooth-rock shapes across the sky.

Quartz snow lay in the patches of shadows, themselves of cold slate sliced from layers of the world's block.

Minerals dripped from the epitite blades of plants.

Birds, limestone fossils, stared out through malachite eyes, as the stone hunters moved by them in the morning's pregnant fluorspar light, sharp as the flint of life.

Somewhere, hidden from the eyes of the hunters, were the deer, cinnabar blood pumping nervousness into each slender, brittle limb.

Finally they were in position. Granla was seen to wave from across the clearing in which the herd was grazing. One or two of the deer had seen the Shaman and instantly their alarm was transmitted throughout the whole herd. Then the beaters rose up in the grass and gave a mighty shout, almost of one accord.

"Hooorahhh!" the sound echoed through the forests. Esk's

soul seemed to swell within his body. Richard, sensing primitive savagery at work and aware of Esk's mind, honed razorsharp by prospect of the coming blood-letting, retreated further from the outside world: he wanted no part of this display of his ancestor's primal lust. The almost overwhelming tremors of excitement running through Esk only served to frighten and confuse the second youth. It was a state of mind outside Richard's understanding.

Several of the deer, on seeing Granla, had broken back, but then the main part of the herd charged forward on hearing the cry of beaters, hoar frost exploding around their hooves. They rolled into one another, one or two leaping high above the shoulders of the pack in an effort to escape the slow centre.

Granla and the other hunters came out on the flanks and threw their spears into the pack. A doe went down, to be trampled by the panic-stricken herd. Esk, running forward still, let loose his spear from the throwing stick: it soared in a beautiful arc but was a second late in reaching its mark. Its point lay buried in a patch of melting snow. Richard missed seeing the failure – he was too far back, his awareness dimmed, almost obliterated, by the potency of Esk's hunt-fever.

Reng said, "You eat what you kill, half-brother. A taste of snow for you tonight."

Esk did not reply but silently wished all the tree and rock spirits in the vicinity might make a concerted attack on Reng and buffet him to death in his bed.

The herd ran on, with the hunters, almost as fast, at their heels. They turned many of the deer, funnelling them into the avenue of inturned stakes. Some escaped, crashing blindly into the forest on either side. One or two jumped the stakes, while others impaled themselves. The majority hurtled over the cliff to their deaths on the rocks below.

A single fawn turned at the entrance to the stakes and headed back for the forest. Esk was retrieving his spear and the fawn danced by him, wide-eyed. It was so close he could smell its fear-sweat and he turned, swiftly executing a beautiful hand throw, transfixing the animal to the ground. Within moments he had slit its throat and began pinning its ankles together with pieces of wood sharpened at both ends. This was his personal kill, to share with no one. He would share also in the group's other kills — the impaled deer and the ones at the foot of the cliff — but a deer felled by his own weapon belonged exclusively to him. He would have his mother make a coat from the skin.

He caught a scowling Reng's eyes and smiled sweetly. Inside the older youth would be eating his heart out, Esk knew.

Richard, dimly conscious now that the hunt was over, began to emerge.

Did you get one?

Of course, bragged Esk to his soul-mate. I am one of the tribe's most talented hunters. I always make a kill.

Not true. This is your second deer only.

You know so much, grumbled Esk. I cannot hide things from you. It may be my second deer but many other creatures have met their deaths at the end of my spear. You should see me with birds! I am the wiliest hunter of birds that ever lived. It is my speciality.

While this rather one-sided interchange had been going on Granla and two other hunters, Neng and Eft, had come to congratulate Esk.

"Well done boy," said Granla with genuine pride in his voice. "If your father were here he would carry your spear home for you as a mark of his esteem for his son. Your father is dead, therefore I will take his place! Give me the weapon. You shall carry your prize." The other two men grinned at him.

Esk's father had recently been trampled to death by a spear-toothed giant. Now Esk had killed one of the children of a tree-head. The Mother had exchanged life for life. He handed his spear to Granla and, with his ego swelling within him (making Richard disgusted with the youth with whom he shared a brain), he started down towards the path that led to the rock shelter. The fawn was soft around his shoulders and warm blood ran down his chest. He was as happy as a caveboy ever could be.

Reng had to remain to help with the storing of the carcasses in the cave, higher up the mountain – which meant he would also have to collect ice in which to pack the meat. He must have been as unhappy as a youth can be, and Esk resolved there and then that Reng would have to be put out of the way soon, for Granla was making an obvious show of the fact that he intended to adopt Esk.

Reng was Granla's son. He would not brook any direct rivalry for leadership, from Esk.

There was a kind of music in the head of Esk that filtered through from Richard, but the infectious happiness of the cave-boy which had caused Richard to come forward and hum lasted only a short while. Richard lapsed into silence and retreated again. He did not like the feel of the grimy body with dried sweat in its creases. Nor did he enjoy the stickiness of the deer's blood around his shoulders and back.

So Esk came forward and attempted to continue the tune but the sophistication of the melody was beyond him and the result was a lapse into the wind-songs and sea-songs of the Paleolithic world – no less complex in their rhythms but of a different musical construction. They sounded like the elements they were meant to represent.

Gradually, as he descended, his instincts began sprouting needles and an unease crept into the soft mouthings. Eventually Esk fell into silence and stared apprehensively around him.

On either side of the path bushes grew with large thorns along their spidery brambles. They threw malevolent-looking shadows over the path ahead. No, he decided, it was not the bushes. Something more than that.

The clack of a wild goat's hoof on stone sounded just a little way off. Then another. They were urgent sounds and Esk sniffed the breeze, trying to classify the danger. All he could smell was the blood of his kill. He shrugged and began to continue his journey. Then he stopped again, abruptly. Something was definitely wrong. It was stupid to ignore it. The unease began to permeate through to Richard, who merely caught the alarming effects and moved further back.

The path dropped sharply in front of Esk forming a small

ledge. He would have to throw down the carcass and climb after it. Something was holding him back, though, and all he could do, until the danger manifested itself into something he could recognize, was to keep perfectly still. Possibilities ran through his mind and Richard cringed mentally as these horrors touched him. He knew Esk was unarmed, save for a knife, and wondered if Reng had followed them.

Esk remained rooted for something like an hour of Richard's clock – an incredible length of time in the view of the modern boy – when finally Esk's patience received payment. A tiny growl came from below the drop. A heavy breathing preceded the cracking of small branches and finally an animal broke cover below the ledge. Esk now knew the danger threatening him. A sloe-eyed juvenile panther was preparing to launch itself up the ledge. Turning into the forest the youth began running for his life.

Drop the deer! Drop the deer! Richard was screaming to the owner of his body. Pain could be left for Esk to enjoy but death would engulf both of them. Richard had already contemplated this eventuality and had decided that while his mind might return to his own body on the death of Esk, it was possible he no longer had a body to go back to. The idea that he might wake up in a decomposing corpse in the blackness of a grave was so horrific it defied imagining. He would rather die in Esk's body than risk that.

Esk was plainly against abandoning his prize even though it might mean his life. Richard read the determination amongst the incoherent thoughts that were scattering through their brain.

Leave it! He tried once more. If he could get to the front he could drop the animal himself, but that would mean taking over command of a situation that was already out of hand. He decided to let Esk deal with it in his own way. The caveboy was, after all, supposed to be the expert.

The ground was soft and the trees impeded the caveboy. Nevertheless he was almost as agile as the panther. At one point the pursuing beast had caught up and with its claws deep into Esk's shoulders it tried to wrest the deer from him. The cat's jaws jerked the meat, shaking it savagely to loosen Esk's grasp.

If Richard thought that the chase was over he was never more wrong. Paleolithic youths did not hand over precious food to panthers without a fight – especially when it was their first big kill. Esk turned his head sharply and bit deeply into the carnivore's foreleg and ground them in until they reached bone.

The panther released the fawn and twisted like a spun rope to free itself from teeth and jaws as strong as a dog's. It left fur and flesh behind and shrieked in pain. Esk was running before the panther's four paws hit the ground.

Ahead of the caveboy, in the roots of a giant tree, was a large hole. The caveboy scrambled down backwards, dragging the fawn behind him, blocking out the light. The Mother had opened Her belly for Her child. She would protect Her potential Shaman from harm. About four feet down the tunnel opened out like a badger's set, into a small cavern. The fawn was jammed sideways in the entrance and while Esk screamed and fought to pull it further into the tunnel, the panther gnawed at the head. There was no other opening to the cramped subterranean hole in which Esk was trapped and consequently there was very little air. Once or twice during the half day that followed the panther tried to pull the deer from the tunnel but Esk fought like a madman to keep it tightly wedged in the opening.

Gradually the air became stale and used and as the night closed the thin cracks around the animal in the tunnel Esk lapsed into a dream-like state. At first he murmured prayers to try to keep himself from slipping into a state of unconsciousness but finally the head that rested beside one of the inadequate ventilation slits lolled sideways. The following morning the frozen white hairs of daylight failed to rouse the caveboy and he lay curled in the underground nest: an unborn Shaman in the womb of Mother Earth.

The predator moved on, melting into the trees.

6

The renegade Neanderthals that had crossed the isthmus from the mainland had not intended to violate the territory of another group but they were hard-pressed. Their wanderings over the continent had resulted in the forced ejection of their group whenever and wherever they stumbled into another group's hunting area. The Cro-Magnons would not often tolerate the presence of the shorter, craggier Neanderthals. They drove them out with a ferocity the Neanderthals could not match.

The group had grown in number as they collected other vagrant families and singles on their travels. By the time they reached their last refuge they were six times larger than the tribe of Homo sapiens that already dwelt on the peninsula. Moreover they were the dregs of their race, being composed of those who were socially unacceptable to the Cro-Magnons, who allowed their ranks to be swollen by Neanderthals, providing the latter were willing to accede to the tribe and abide by any established rules.

Even though they were a motley, aggressive group of men, however, they had grown tired of expulsion and wanted nothing more than to find a free stretch of land where they could keep their own peace – or not, as they wished. Their Shaman was called Skell and his leadership was exceptional. Without him they would have divided or perished long before. He had pushed them over waterless deserts and pulled them over frozen blocks of mountains.

Physically Skell was no stronger than the average man of his particular group. There were larger, tougher men. Others could be fiercer in battle. It was Skell's personality that was his strength. He had the ability to turn the power of others to his

85

own uses. Someone was always by his side – a protector. Sometimes the protector's and antagonist's roles were reversed but he never stood alone.

Skell could drive fear into a man's heart with an expression or a few low-voiced phrases. His voice was harsh and guttural, and his words could carry hooded, mysterious threats which were difficult to interpret but evident enough to disturb the sleep of the recipient. His magic was awesome. Rivals disappeared, during darkness, without a trace. When accused of their abduction he would ask, "By whom?" His accusers would search in vain for the missing agents of the Shaman, only to find their implied evidence present.

Malcontents had been known to awaken, after sleeping with a friend on either side, to find a hand, or, worse still, a foot missing, the stump burned to prevent haemorrhaging. No immediate pain – just the loss of an irretrievable appendage. The pain came later.

In all cases the victims had sat with Skell late into the night, by his fire, and listened to his arguments until they were ragged with tiredness and crept away to sleep.

Skell was a gifted hypnotist. His name meant "eyes in the skull".

The Shaman's main ally was a man from the Land of Greyclouds called Crak. An intelligent fighter and a born lieutenant, Crak bore the scars of many defences of his leader's policies, the most awesome of which was a hole in his left cheek through which he could poke his tongue. Caused by a spear wound, bubbles of spittle formed and burst on that place to the side of the great dome head whenever he grew angry, until rivulets of saliva ran down the heavy jaw and wet the ground below. Crak would stand, his thick, hairy arms dangling from rounded shoulders, and his brow jutting forward, threatening to splinter an opponent's bones once he caught hold of him (which was how he earned his name). That he rarely bothered to pursue a foe beyond a dozen stamped-out yards did not injure his reputation. His one attack upon the yielding skeleton of an enemy was within recent memory.

It had been an unlucky *new-man* hunter that attempted to stop the group from stealing his long-stalked and hard-killed bison. He made the mistake of throwing out a challenge, which, though not understood in words, was not difficult to interpret from tone and gesture. The hunter had stood his ground, tall and sure of his skill, when Crak had lumbered out of the group and walked weaponless into his spear. The wooden lance with its flake-tipped point skidded from the stocky Crak's rib-cage and buried its flint in the right arm, just above the elbow.

Crak had merely grunted, the impact of the missile hardly breaking his stride. Even Skell had felt the fear well up in his throat when his lieutenant grasped the courageous hunter by the shoulders and drove a knee like a tree-stump into his sternum. All heard the crack. All saw the blood-vomit. None cared for similar treatment.

The wanderings of Skell's group had its origin in the far north where several unusually bitter winters had driven many ice-dwellers southwards, sometimes into the territory of a strange, tall people with erect postures and often unfriendly attitudes. The Tall Ones, unlike the Northerners, lived in caves and rock shelters, and their clothes fitted around their bodies rather than hung over them in the drape-like fashion of Skell's people. Confrontations were many, and several of Skell's women deserted this camp to enter the comfortable caves of the arrogant Southerners. This did not, of course, endear the roving hunters, already envious and bewildered, to the cave-dwellers. They hunched their large heads even deeper into their shoulders and glowered when they saw the hill-fires of their newly found enemies. Their small eyes glared from beneath the beetle brows, not guessing that theirs was a species doomed, if not to complete extinction, at least to a melting-away by integration to form a barely detectable element in a compound race.

Skell realized by the night fires reported to him by his men, that he had not found a vacant paradise for his people. He wisely did not attempt to make contact with the group on the coast, preferring instead to take his people high up the snow-covered slopes of the mountains into the colder air which re-minded him of his original home. Some of his men complained that there was more food to be had on the lowlands but he refuse to be swayed from his decision. There was plenty of game to be seen on the high ground, he argued; sheep and deer. They were as well off there as anywhere. Also, he said, thickly wooded mountains were good places to defend. You could see your enemy coming from a long way off and there was plenty of cover if a battle should prove inevitable.

Some of them grumbled but as usual relented. No one wanted to make the climb with a missing foot. Or a broken leg.

Skell always began his day by feeling either "useful" or "of no use". He was never depressed, bad-tempered, in a foul mood, happy, cheerful or ecstatic, although his language had adjectives to match all these feelings. Degrees of his mood were expressed by varying the phrases. "Of little use" was a mood which could be tolerated by both himself and his followers but "as useful as a sick insect" was an ugly, black mood of which to beware.

"Useful" also described Skell's confidence when faced with problematical situations. Crak did not do all the disciplining for his leader. If Skell felt "useful" he would take on the task himself and let any adversary beware when Skell said to Crak, "I will deal with this man. I feel I could be useful in a fight today." For Skell, as a winner, could be far more cruel than his lieutenant. He was the type of man who believed that if you had your opponent on the floor, to let him get up again would be a mistake.

Since his appetite for women was virtually bottomless op-ponents were not rare and he could afford to be selective – as he needed to be, since he was, after all, only of ordinary size and weight for a Northerner.

The day they woke in the pine forest on the slopes of the crisp, white mountain Skell felt useful. He slapped the belly of his sleeping bed-mate playfully and she woke with a jump, her yellow teeth chattering in confusion.

"What is it? What is it?" she cried, looking round for the

animal-skin cover which Skell had pulled from her nakedness.

"It is a day," he said. "A white day. A day that jangles the bones in our bodies. Get up and greet this extraordinary day."

She stared at the grinning Shaman, teeth still clacking, and he attempted to gauge what her reaction would be. She had antagonized him the night before by slamming her thighs together too sharply and temporarily damaging his manhood. The subsequent tender nursing she had administered had saved her from an immediate beating but retribution could still be administered. It was a fact that the shock to the Shaman's system the night before had been part of the reason why no punishment had been meted out. All he had wanted to do was curl up with his agony for an hour – and afterwards the caressing had begun.

She seemed happy.

"It's a good day isn't it?" she replied, pulling on her body fur and he knew he would let her return to her regular man soon.

"A very good day," he said, watching the eclipse of white skin with interest. "We shall make our base here. I shall see to it that we build some shelters from branches and skins to keep out the snow. I like snow when it's crisp and dry but in the thaw it chills with its dampness. I'm not pleased with slush for a bed. I don't feel very useful when I wake in a pool of ice-water."

"Shall I ask a man to make a fire? Then I can cook you some food." She seemed anxious to be out of the sphere of his attention and unfortunately for her it showed.

He growled something at her and she scuttled away. Then he gathered those of his men who were currently in favour around him and told them what they must do. There was little discussion: Skell was a dictator who believed that discussion only led to split decisions. The most immediate problem was food and the majority of the men were assigned to hunting for the day. Once they had left, several others took out their fire-making tools and competed with one another to be the first to bring forth the flame. Once the bright, life-preserving element was produced it was transferred to a pile of dry grasses which the Northerners carried with them wrapped in animal skins. Semi-dry local wood was placed on this and it was not too long before a roaring bonfire was roasting the midriffs of hungry men and women. Flames do not fill a stomach but they warm the spirit which lives inside it. Northerners believed the prime organ of the body was the stomach. The heart, centre of anatomical attention for future generations, was of little interest to them.

The stomach was the symbol of life. You filled it and you grew strong. You left it empty and you weakened. It was positioned in the centre of the body, therefore all else radiated from the stomach. It was unprotected by a cage of bones and was therefore vulnerable in battle. A stomach could govern your moods. If it pained, life could be miserable. A common greeting asked, "How is your stomach today?" You fell in love through your stomach. The heart was merely a sac full of blood. (Northerners were as familiar with the physical human form, inside and out, as any man could be. They had cut enough of them up in their time and had a natural curiosity.)

Once several days had passed on the snowbound ledges of the mountains, the Northerners persuaded their Shaman that life would embrace them a lot less coldly further down the slopes in the green foothills. They did not all originate in the north, they argued, and many of them were falling ill of rheumatic diseases. Skell maintained that the cold air was a lot more healthy than the warmer air of the valleys but agreed to a compromise. The unfortunate aspect of the movements was that their search for an ideal home took them ever closer to the *new-men* group. Finally they arrived in a place at the foot of the island's largest mountain, some twenty miles away from the natives. One of Skell's scouts came charging up to the Shaman with the typical Northern gracefulness likened by the Tall Ones to a boar suffering from toothache.

"A cave. I have found a cave," he told Skell excitedly. The

man's name was Elk. Normally he was unresponsive and dull. Skell was at a loss to understand why he was so enthusiastic. He asked guardedly, "Is there a bear in it?" The Northern word for bear was "knife-paw", and there was a great value placed on the beast's hide, teeth and claws. They were, as Skell well knew, however, very difficult and dangerous beasts to kill.

"No," said Elk, his smile becoming wider still and his pleasure glowing visibly through his broad face.

Skell shook his head, puzzled.

"Then I fail to share your joy. Why should I be enthusiastic over a hole in the rock?"

"Don't you see," said the insistent Elk. "We can live like the Tall Ones — inside a cave. It's a large cave. Some of us could sleep around the entrance . . ."

He stopped, seeing Skell's expression change.

"What's the matter?"

"Yes . . . like the Tall Ones. Show me this cave."

Elk eagerly led the way through the trees until, about a mile from the group, they came to a sheer-faced cliff at the foot of which was a large cave entrance. It was a difficult spot to find since the trees masked the tooth-like cliff from a frontal view. Elk had found the place by accident. He explained that he had been walking along the green-brown slope which merged into the side of the cliff when he had slipped on a wet patch of grass and slid down the steep slope. Picking himself up unharmed he had tried to climb up again but found the scree on the slope too loose. Finally he had given up, walked along the foot of the rock spur that took over from the earth-covered ridge. That was when he discovered the cave.

To Skell it looked like a ghoul's open mouth in an eyeless face — it frightened him. He knew that several of the North-erners had already lived in caves and after some reassurance he entered. It smelt damp and musty inside the mouth and Skell prayed fervently to the gods of the rocks to keep him from harm — silently, of course, for Elk seemed quite at ease: he was one of those who had already lived inside the throat of the earth.

"This is . . ." began Skell, staring fearfully into a blackness that was thicker and more deadly than midnight with no moon.

A voice called back to him, hollowly. The voice of a demon or a dead man, still walking. The place was evil: a gathering-hole for malevolent phantoms.

"Ahhhhh!" screamed Skell, turning to run, and the demon shrieked back in the same coarse tones, following Skell out into the sunlight.

Skell ran until he was standing in the stream which the two men had passed earlier and he splashed in its clear water, shivering with terror. The demon could not follow him into water or fire. Fire was a better protection but he could hardly ring himself with flames at a moment's notice. The water would have to do.

He was amazed and highly suspicious when a calm Elk came strolling out of the trees. Skell had been sure the demon would have eaten his follower by now. Perhaps the demon had assumed Elk's form?

"Stop!" commanded the Shaman.

Elk's form halted in its tracks.

"What's my name?" enquired Skell craftily.

"Your name?" asked the demon, trying to appear puzzled but only succeeding in looking sly.

"Yes, my name? And your name? What are both our names, you slimy sputum from the throat of a ghoul?"

The evil spirit in the guise of Elk began to look angry.

"Why call me names, Skell? You're the Shaman but you have no right to insult me – by the beard of my sister I'm as entitled to honour as any man. . . ."

"And your name?" asked Skell, not wavering until he was sure.

"Elk! Elk! My name is Elk," shouted what truly must have been the Northern scout, for a demon will always become confused with human names, and either mispronounce them or forget them altogether.

Mollified, but still on his guard, Skell stepped from the water. He asked his comrade, "How did you escape the demon? The one that shouted death at us with its foul stinking breath?"

Elk's expression changed and a light appeared in his eyes.

"You mean . . . that's no demon. It's a *good* spirit that always sends your own words back to you – so that they're not lost in the underworld, to be stolen by bad spirits. Only *good* spirits inhabit caves, Shaman. It's too close to the surface for demons."

Skell felt ashamed. "How was I supposed to know that?" he grumbled. "I've never lived in caves before."

In an innocent tone Elk replied, "You *are* the Shaman." The implication being that the Shaman knew all things.

Skell declined to answer and would have promised the insolent scout a thrashing to be administered by Crak, except that if he did he would have nothing to hold over the man to prevent Skell's cowardly actions of the afternoon reaching other ears. They both knew it had to remain a secret.

The two men returned to the group and led them back to the cave, Skell silently reassuring himself that he need not sleep inside the hated mouth – he could use his love of cold, fresh air as an excuse to stay outside. Crak could sleep inside, within earshot of the young men, to prevent the emergence of any conspiracy. The politics of power were a heavy burden. The power itself, however, was delightful and worth risking his lieutenant's soul for, if not his own.

The latter part of the day brought another discovery – torches taken into the cave revealed the walls to be decorated with paintings. Once more Skell had to enter the hated tunnel and, though it was not so fearful with the torchlight chasing away the darkness around him, he was even more convinced that these were the jaws of the mountain. Running saliva joined the roof and floor of the cave and white teeth protruded from both upper and lower parts of the mouth. He skirted the larger ones gingerly, having a mental picture of the jaws coming violently together and masticating the whole group. He was happy to see he was not the only one ill at ease. Looking round he could see the sweat clearly on the brows of several other claustrophobic Northerners.

In the huge cavern behind the mouth he found the paintings and stared at them in wonder. He too was an artist but not as skilled as the author of these pictures of deer and hunters, and wild pigs, their legs stick-like and pointing to heaven in death.

"This is a magic place," he said, whispering softly so that the spirit would not need to throw back his words – good or bad.

"A Shaman has this place for his holy rites. If we dig here we will find bodies – or skeletons – of the Tall Ones. This is a holy place. . . ."

"It's a safe, dry place," said someone, unconsciously whispering like his leader. They were afraid Skell would order another move.

"We are not afraid of the Tall Ones."

"Don't worry," replied Skell, "we shall stay here. It will give us the opportunity to capture the Shaman of the group on the coast. With him in our hands we shall have a decided advantage over the rest of his men – they will be robbed of their magician. Soon we shall own the whole piece of land beyond the thin sands. . . ."

At this a loud cheer went up from his relieved people, which rolled round inside the vault in a seemingly never-ending thunderous growl, and it was all Skell could do to smile weakly and stop his legs from running his terrified body out into the sweet, unwalled air under the blue sky.

7

Levan threw the skull hard against the garage wall and watched the impact break the bone into two halves. Had it not been coated in resilient plastic it would have shattered into a thousand pieces.

"That was bloody stupid," he said to himself. Smashing his Paleolithic skeletons wouldn't cure his son. He had been brooding over the pile of bones, blaming himself and his long-dead ancestors for Richard's illness. Or was it an illness? He didn't know. He knew nothing very much any more.

That morning, after a long sleepless night, he had looked into the cracked bedroom mirror of the rented flat and had seen an unshaven face, gaunt cheeks, soot-ringed eyes. Not very pleasant. He had then returned to his bungalow after a quick visit to Richard (which revealed that there had been no change in the boy) to make sure Kariyos was coping with things in Kyrenia. He needn't have worried, of course – Kariyos was quite capable. He had then checked his mail. On the screen in his study was a growing pile of offers from collectors of Pale-ontologic remains, but they held no interest for him. All he wanted now was his son returned.

"That hardnut doctor," Levan muttered, picking up the two hemispheres of the skull. "I'll give him one more day. One more. Then I send Richard to the States. Should have done that in the first place."

Richard had been mindless for only four days but to Levan it seemed very much longer. He had little patience. A tragedy such as the one he was experiencing lay on his mind every waking minute. Time pulled itself along with heavy legs.

The garage door slid open and a worried, grizzled coun-tenance appeared round its edge.

Levan sighed, nodding at the weathered old Greek. "I'm sorry — yes, I'm okay. I . . . I had an accident. Broke a bone. . . ."

There was an answering frown.

"You broke bone — where? You hurt?"

"No, no. Not hurt. It was one of the old bones. Don't worry."

A grave nod from Kariyos.

"Okay, but you got a visitor. In the house."

Hell, not that bastard McKinnon, thought Levan. The man had only been on the island two days and already Levan detested him. Or had he already hated him before he had arrived? It was difficult to remember as far back as four days. He must have loathed him because he could remember Loraine introducing them at the hospital while he was watching over Richard's staring form. He had felt the squirming worms of dislike in his stomach even before looking up to shake hands. What the hell she had thought she was doing, bringing her ex-husband to meet her lover, was beyond Levan.

"What's he look like? It is a he?"

"I know him — that man with a girl's face. The professor," explained Kariyos disdainfully.

Levan said, "Ah!" and went immediately through the side door that led directly into the bungalow. Leidermann was propped up in a tall-backed locally made chair and he looked very uncomfortable. He sprang to his feet on Levan's approach, extending his hand.

"Mr Levan, how are you? Is there any improvement?"

He was plainly nervous and although Levan still held the American partly responsible he felt he had taken that side of things far enough for the present. He shook the professor's hand.

"I'm fine — oh yes, I really am. I know I look ghastly. . . ." Now why did he use an adjective like that? He had never used words like "ghastly" before in his life. "Richard's pretty much the same though. I'm glad you've come — I want to ask you a few things. Questions. Do you mind? I was very uncivil last time," he continued.

"Of course," replied Leidermann in a relieved tone. "By all

means. I must admit I was a little apprehensive about coming here. I thought you might ... well, frankly, I thought you might throw me out. But I had to come. We *are* partly responsible – I realize that, though I'm afraid I would deny it in court. My associates, you see. . . ."

Levan stiffened for a moment, feeling the anger well up again in his breast, but then remembered that the bone of contention, even if resolved in his favour, could only mean financial recompense. He wanted his boy whole again. Money was of little use to a mindless cabbage.

"Let's go for a walk," suggested Levan. "I hate this room."

"As you wish."

They left the bungalow by the back door. Levan did not want to pass Loraine's house with McKinnon there. Rosemary had gone to visit Richard and Levan felt he might be tempted to look in, on the way past. He would have wondered what they were doing, now that they were alone, except that he was torturing himself enough already. It was an easy thing to get used to, this racking of one's own soul, thought Levan. Perhaps some men even enjoyed it?

"Mr Levan?" Leidermann was looking at him. They were crossing a dry stream bed. In the winter rains it was full of wild, torrential water which cut deeply into the earth baring the rocks beneath. Leidermann was having difficulty walking over them in his slippery-soled city shoes.

"Sorry," said Levan. "Here, let's go up on that grassy hillock – at least, it's grass some of the year round."

They scrambled to the spot with difficulty, only to find the ground covered in thorns. It was the dry season. The bushes and plants were now brittle and sharp to touch. Pliable when green, they pierced even the thickest clothes in the summer. There were also large ants all over the place.

"What was it you wished to know, Mr Levan?" He made no attempt to sit down.

"Paul, please, Professor," he replied absently.

"Paul."

"Well," said Levan earnestly, "I want to know something

97

about the repeater — how it works. It might give someone a clue about why Richard . . . well, it just might help."

Leidermann pursed his lips and Levan thought for a moment he was going to refuse to answer. The Wiederhaus Repeater had an aura of mystery which Leidermann's "associates" wanted to retain.

Levan said, "Look, Leidermann — I want to know how it works, what the cogs and spindles, or their equivalents, do on that damned machine. You have some idea. . . ."

The answer was preceded by a slow nod and then Leidermann explained, "It's a light wave receiver, influenced to some degree by currents produced from the Earth's magnetic field. Reproducing pictures of the past — actual scenes as it were — that it extracts from the wave patterns it picks up. Everything living has presence — emits energy which is never lost, wholly. There are pressure lines in the force field which the repeater gathers to its banks and it takes these wave fragments of the past, analyses them for physical formation — size and shape of the body from which the energy was produced — and forms a three-dimensional picture. . . ."

"That's all a bit beyond me, Leidermann — what the hell have all these little . . ." (Levan imagined small, barely visible worms rippling in the air above his diggings) ". . . these wavelets been doing for thirty-five thousand years? Waiting to be hooked?"

"Wave *forms*, not wavelets. Well, they're just there — vibrations in the rocks — the rhythms of time which are part of the previously uncovered earth. Personally I have my own ideas. Technology this close to witchcraft is not to my taste. . . ."

Levan considered this for a moment, then shook his head. "I paid to see three-dimensional pictures of the past. I had no idea they actually *came* from the past. I thought — well, frankly, I thought it was ghosting."

"It is. . . ."

"But you don't believe in it?"

"Yeah. Oh, sure, the energy is there — *but in a different form*. I think the source is the same — the energy of past living creatures – but the state of that energy is where I disagree with the official explanation. My version would frighten people too much – scare them away from using the repeater. A magnetic field is a physical presence people understand – the lodestone world – they know that, or at least they believe the circumstantial evidence; the Earth's magnetic field exists, light waves can be seen."

Levan thought for a moment, then said in an exasperated tone, "But, what about the timing? And the accuracy? I mean, why use the skeletons? It doesn't make sense."

"Doesn't make sense. That's what I said," replied the professor, "when I first heard it. And I still say it. Sometimes I get the feeling I'm being conned, but what else can I say? It works. Perhaps that story is a whitewash to cover the *real truth*."

Levan deliberately ignored the innuendos.

"And what about the witchery with the skeletons?"

Leidermann shrugged. "Alex Wiederhaus calls it 'local time flavouring' and when he does try to discuss it, it seems a bit like black magic. Something about the emission of age rays from *within the bones* causing an attractive quality which aids the receiver. A kind of fine tuning, I suppose. Can you grasp that?"

"Not unless you explain what these 'age rays' are and what they consist of."

"I can't do that. Not because I don't want to but because I don't know. The whole theory – and practice – sounds like it's been snaffled from the Book of Witchcraft. But, I repeat – it works. I can't dispute it, so I accept it for what it is. *Officially.* . . . In the case of your son we add a new dimension to the machine. It must create a magnetic attraction between two minds held apart by time – when brought into contact they snap together – the unlike poles of magnets. *Crack.* Like that. Lodestone brothers. . . ."

"I still don't understand how you can work the thing and still pretend to know so little about it."

Leidermann shrugged. "Can't you? Why should an operator share the technician's knowledge? Taxi drivers don't have to

99

know how their machine works — they just need to know how to drive it. That's hardly a parallel but you get the idea? The receiver's frequencies are pre-set by my brother-in-law before it arrives. All I have to do is make some minor adjustments and switch on. Myself, I have another theory about the repeater . . . an *unofficial* theory." His voice had a cracked note to it. He seemed to be falling into an emotional state.

"Yes?"

"You mentioned ghosting — I think you hit it on the head. I believe the repeater bridges the gap between the physical world and the supernatural. . . ." Leidermann's eyes were unusually alive and Levan felt uncomfortable. A prickling sensation made his skin itch all over.

"Don't be silly," Levan said, swallowing.

"No, really," continued the professor in the same feverish tones. "Perhaps those tubes are the first of a long line of mediums — a computerized spiritualist. Not a receiver of physical rays, but waves from beyond our space and time — from the world of the dead. . . ."

Stumbling a little, Levan backed away from the little man with the earnest expression, muttering, "Jesus. Jesus," under his breath, and really meaning it for once. Then he quickly led the way down to the bungalow below where his tired mind might find a little sanity. Was the whole world mad? He had sought out his remote Kyrenian sanctuary to get away from the madmen. Now they followed him here. Emma, why did you leave me? he silently cried.

Leidermann left, after promising to contact Weiderhaus to ask the inventor if he could help in any way. Levan remained in his bungalow surrounded by tapes on psychology and psychiatry — the remains of an attempt to find a solution to his son's problem. There was even a cartridge of films on brain surgery. He sat bolt upright, staring into space for a while, before slipping imperceptibly into the half-awake state which exhaustion induces. After an hour had passed the visiphone brought him out of his trance. Someone was calling him.

"Paul? This is Rosemary. Rosemary McKinnon." She was always very correct on the visiphone, but her voice was laden with excitement.

"Paul, I'm at the hospital. Richard *spoke* to me. . . ." The last words came out in a rush. "Isn't that wonderful? The doctor said I could call you and tell you. He's here now." Her picture faded and was replaced by that of the young doctor.

"What?" mumbled Levan. His brain was buzzing and he was confused. He had crossed his tiredness threshold twice over and was finding it difficult to comprehend now that he had allowed himself to begin sinking into that deep pit of unconsciousness following exhaustion.

"What?" He tried to scratch his chin as the image in front of him began talking. The hand came up but his co-ordination was gone.

". . . Richard's sitting up and he seems fully conscious. Mr Levan? Are you all right?"

Richard well again? This time the words did get through and he felt their impact on his mind. Bursting into tears Levan sobbed that he was fine and that after a couple of hours rest, he would leave for the hospital. He wanted to go immediately but knew he couldn't make the journey in his present state. He collapsed onto the thick pile carpet and fell into a fitful, dream-interrupted sleep.

Loraine had travelled to Cyprus for the seclusion she hoped it would offer after her marriage to McKinnon broke up. It was the second side of a triangle she had begun drawing with her travels when she left Scotland with her new husband to begin a life in Canada. She hoped one day to complete the triangle by returning to Scotland, but not yet. She liked the climate of Cyprus too much to leave until she was old and infirm. Then she would make that nostalgic journey back to her homeland.

She had met McKinnon at a local dance in the village of Logieard. He was a second generation Canadian who *had* made the pilgrimage back to the land of his forefathers. Loraine had pulled him easily — too easily. They were married within a month of meeting and the fighting began not long afterwards. She, the Scottish wild-cat, and he the forest bear. They were a match for one another in that the cat knows just how much tormenting the bear will take before it loses its temper. She kept him on the edge, constantly, until she either wore him down and got her way, or until he landed a blow which softened her attitude. She was quicker and more spiteful. He was heavy.

Loraine was lying on the portable beach bed on the balcony when Rosemary called her and told her the good news. Alan was in the local bar and Loraine debated with herself on whether it was best to see him first and take her ex-husband with her to see Paul, or whether to go alone. On the one hand she knew that if Alan accompanied her there might be trouble between the two men — they had met at the hospital briefly and she noticed their immediate antipathy. On the other hand, if she went alone Paul might insist they make love and she couldn't do that with Alan so close. She decided that Paul would be feeling better now that Richard had recovered and it would be a good time to reintroduce the two men. She half-wondered to herself whether or not she was enjoying the prospect of having her two men facing each other. She thought that even at her mature age she would be disappointed if one of them didn't show a little jealousy.

"Beautiful girl," said a voice from the doorway.

She had not heard it slide open. Her choice was made for her. Alan had returned from his lunchtime session with the locals in the bar. He was not displaying any signs of drunkenness but she knew he would have over-indulged — he always did. He had a large capacity, however, and it was only when he had to carry out some task that required precision that his inebriation became evident.

"Beautiful girl," he repeated, this time with just a trace of thickness in the voice. The first time had required training. She had not let Alan touch her since he had arrived and she had no intention, now that he was on Cyprus, of allowing him to do so.

He might take it, she knew, but she thought not. When he had been in Canada, she wanted *him*. Now that he was here, she needed Paul.

"Richard's better," she said quickly, tossing some loose strands of hair over her shoulder. She was wearing jeans with a tee-shirt tucked in the waistband. She knew Alan liked tight clothes. Was she unconsciously trying to provoke him?

"Ah, good," he said, not really comprehending. "That's young Rosemary's boyfriend."

"Paul's son. I told you. The lad had an accident a few days ago."

"Yes, yes. Partly the reason I flew here wasn't it?" He sounded irritable.

Was that the reason Alan had come? She could not remember whether she had told him about Richard before or after his decision to travel to Cyprus.

"I'm just going over to Paul's bungalow – Rosemary said he came back to look at his mail. You can come too, if you wish."

"If I wish?" he mocked her voice, exaggerating the feminine pitch. He put a hand on her shoulder and she knocked it away, saying vehemently, "Dinna touch me." Occasionally the Scottish accent, which had been anglicized by school years in London, came through thick and strong.

"Wouldn't dream of it, sugar," he said, smiling dangerously. She ducked beneath his still outstretched arm and made it through the door and into the sunlight before he caught up with her.

"Pretty quick for an old bag," he said, annoyed at being thwarted.

This time she smiled.

"Oh, I know you McKinnon. You couldn't catch a hobbled granny when you're drunk."

He snorted and shrugged, stopping for a moment in his tracks. Then he followed her from a distance of thirty yards. She knew why. Alan wanted her to prepare Paul for him before he strolled up and took the measure of his opponent.

Richard was thankful that Esk was asleep. He felt sure the caveboy would be terrified when he awoke and found himself in the modern world. Richard tried to visualize the room through Esk's eyes, but failed. All he could feel at the time was the enormous relief at being free from the hole under the roots of the tree.

"Are you all right?" asked Rosmary for the tenth time. She was wearing a white tennis top and claret skirt. On her feet she had tennis shoes and white socks. She looked what she was: clean, pink-skinned and as fragrant as white lilac. The comparison between her and the cavegirls was astonishing. They belonged to different worlds, thought Richard. Then mentally winced – of course they did.

"Did you hear me *boy*?" she said.

"Yes, sorry. I'm okay." He was very fond of Rosemary and seeing her, like this, when he had not expected to ever again, gave him a deep feeling of pleasure.

"Well you don't look it. You look flayed."

"I'm okay," he repeated laconically. He wondered when Esk would wake. Richard had brought them to the present time by sheer will-power. In the hole it seemed that they should unequivocally die of suffocation. He had at first fought against the thought of death, then, accepting it, had felt an overwhelming pang of homesickness rush through his body. The longing for his own time had been the vehicle which carried them forward to make the wish reality.

The door to the room slid open and a haggard-looking form entered.

"Richard – you're okay?"

"Dad!" Richard drawled the word in embarrassment. "I've told everyone from the hospital cat upwards – I'm as good as new."

Levan looked puzzled. "Cat?" Then he realized it was a joke and tried to laugh. It came out as a croak.

It was Rosemary who expressed the feelings of both the adolescents.

"Stim, you look like death. It's Richard who's supposed to be ill."

Levan ran his fingers through his uncombed hair.

"Yes. I suppose I do. I've just woken up. Look, Rosemary — your mother and father are down in reception. Would you mind . . .?"

Rosemary looked a little flustered.

"No, no. 'Course not. See you Rick. Later okay?"

She hesitated, then kissed him quickly, on the cheek.

"Okay," replied Richard, disappointed that she had to leave him. It was a new experience for him, having Rosemary fuss over his sickbed. He had been enjoying it — now that everything was back to normal.

When she had gone he said to his father, "She's right, Dad, you look terrible. I expect you've been hanging around here waiting for me to surface?"

"Some of the time. Anyway." Levan gave him a tired nod and a grin. "You look pretty fit to me now."

"I *feel* okay," replied Richard slowly.

The inference was lost on the weary father. "The stamina of youth. I could do with some fitness myself. Have you seen the doctors yet? Will they let you go home?"

"I don't know," said Richard, not wanting to look at his father's puffed red-veined eyes. They made him feel guilty for some reason.

"Okay," said Levan, touching his hair. "Let's ask them." He left the room for a few minutes but was soon back.

Richard asked, "What does the doctor say. Can I go home?"

"One more night. If everything goes well you can come home tomorrow — but you'll have to have some regular check-ups — maybe daily."

"I don't mind." He was wondering whether to tell his father about Esk, before the Paleolithic youth awoke.

"Dad," he said cautiously. "Do people — well, do they go crazy after an experience like mine?"

Levan looked at him sharply.

"Why do you say that?"

"Well, thing is, I feel I've been somewhere. . . ."

"Of course you do. Thousands of fantasies must have been running through your mind while you've been lying there. God, it's been *days* son. They're just dreams. Don't worry about them. . . ."

Richard decided to be frank with his father.

"I *have* been somewhere, Dad. A long way back into the time when those men lived – those skeletons. . . ."

A worried frown appeared on the adult's face.

"I don't think so, son," said his father. "Dreams can seem very real . . . I once had a fever and – well, the dreams were quite vivid." He looked around as if he expected someone to call him a liar any second.

"But someone came back with me, Dad," insisted Richard. "That's how I know it's not a dream – he's here with me, in my head . . ." Richard paused.

Levan was pale and his eyes looked even more frighteningly red against the paste-coloured skin of his face.

"No," he replied. "I'm sorry if I seem dense, son, but at this time I would rather you didn't say anything to the hospital staff about these experiences . . . the after-effects of fever – they seem real enough, I know, but time will show . . ."

"But I haven't had a fever, Dad!"

At that moment the doctor entered and both of them fell silent. Richard prepared himself for the medical interrogation that was to follow. He had already been through such an ordeal earlier that day. He was beginning to learn the ropes. Don't mention Pleistocene journeys. Don't mention wild, primitive youths asleep at the back of your skull, ready to spring awake and scream incoherently through the thin walls of your mind. Only mad people have such tales to tell. . . .

"Schizophrenia," said Levan later to McKinnon and Loraine in the haven of his rented flat. "After the doctor left he insisted once again that he had brought someone back with him from the past – another boy. The one from the hologram . . . he must be ill."

"Maybe the kid's telling the truth," replied McKinnon, sitting awkwardly on the arm of Loraine's chair.

"Don't be stupid," said Levan. "I want sensible suggestions — some advice."

McKinnon looked at Levan dangerously and said, "He's your goddam son. Why are you asking our advice?"

"I'm not asking you — I'm asking her."

He pointed to Loraine, while still looking at McKinnon. "You don't count."

She quickly intervened.

"Cool down, both of you. God, you're a pair of children yourselves. I'm inclined to agree with Alan, though, Paul. What he means is that Richard's reality may be different from ours. He's just experienced an accident no other person on this earth has gone through."

She settled back into the chair, untucking her legs from beneath her.

"Think of this," she said. "You asked Leidermann how the repeater functioned and he gave you two different answers — an official one which he did not believe in himself, and his own personal theory. But," she emphasized the word, "in both cases he referred to the repeater as a 'receiver' of some sort of energy, either physical or spiritual. What if, in touching the machine, Richard short-circuited those waves, rays, or whatever they are? Perhaps he acted as an earth and they flowed through him instead of taking an unnatural path through the repeater?"

Levan saw some sense in this argument. Loraine continued. "So, those three-dimensional pictures would be received by Richard's brain — he would be 'transported', in his own mind, back to — when was it?"

"The late Pleistocene Age," replied Levan. "So perhaps these scenes — real to Richard in his own mind — don't necessarily mean he's crazy. He's just got a different slant on reality. . . ."

McKinnon made a sound as if he was amused by something.

"What's the matter?" asked Loraine.

He shook his head, saying, "I was just wondering what the

definition of madness was. I mean, you could say — no, never mind."

Loraine was glaring at him but Levan sighed and stood up. "No, he's right, Loraine. If the boy is divorced from reality then he's mentally ill — there's no way of escaping that. I'll have a talk to him, when I pick him up tomorrow, though what that will do I don't know. He seemed pretty convinced today." Levan changed tack. "Where are you staying, McKinnon? Can I give you a lift?"

"I'll make my own way back to my hotel," said McKinnon. He turned to Loraine. "I want to see my kid before I turn in — I've hardly seen anything of her since I've been here."

"It's her choice, not mine," came the reply. "She'll be asleep now, anyway. See her tomorrow."

After he had left Levan and Loraine alone, she said, "He's been asking about the skeletons. I think he needs money, needs it desperately. Wanted to know if you'd an agent. I think he fancies the job. . . ."

Levan replied angrily. "He must be crazy. I've got no job, nothing for him."

"Does that include me?"

McKinnon was on his way back to Kyrenia by skipboat. He had decided against a taxi in favour of water transport. The night was a warm one and he sat on the deck with a drink in his hand thinking about Levan — or rather about Levan's assets. If he could get his hands on just one of those skeletons he could stall the debt collectors for long enough to be able to find a new identity. He couldn't get hold of the whole chunk, that was for sure. He had dropped too much this time. All he wanted was enough to allay any fear that he was going to slip into the Oriental Maze. Even so it was a hell of a lot of money and Levan had not exactly taken to his girlfriend's ex-husband. Still some time in hand yet. He could enjoy the air around him a little longer, he thought.

The skippers beneath the boat flicked water globules high into the evening sky as it raced through the sea. Some of them were as large as the crystal balls used by fortune-tellers. They caught the light of the stars in their lucid forms, then elongated and fell, each trapped star becoming a bright ovum of unborn life in a transparent fecund egg. Then the eggs broke up into drops of plasma before bursting on the surface in the wake of the boat.

McKinnon's thoughts turned towards the events of the day. He was no nearer to solving his financial problems, but he got a kick from coming into contact with men like Levan. They lived in a different world – an innocent world. He was sure that both Levan and his son would simply dismiss the thought that either of them would be capable of even the pettiest theft.

But at least, he thought, gambling was cleaner and healthier than most of the vices he could name. And when it did become unhealthy or fatal, it was not the actual highs and lows of the *main game* that did the damage – as with drugs – it was the lack of resources which led to broken backs or limbs.

He shuddered, suddenly, thinking of his own predicament.

The innocence of Levan had not been earned, though. He was not a *better* man than McKinnon, just a luckier one. If Levan had been born the son of a lumberjack with a liking for crude moonshine, and had made his mark in spite of it, then he could look down on McKinnon in distaste. As it was he had been introduced into the world with full pockets. Steely unbendable principles tempered by a strong family background had been handed on to him. McKinnon's principles were well and truly battered and kinked by the time he was old enough to recognize them and it would have been a man with more stamina than he that took them on the long walk back to the forge to attempt to straighten them.

That Levan boy. What was it he had said to his old man? Been back to the Stone Age? The machinations of some kids' minds defied the imagination, thought McKinnon, taking another sip of his drink and idly spying on a couple of young dressed-for-the-evening lovers fondling each other by the rail.

Maybe Loraine's idea had something? Perhaps the boy was a

victim of the machine, the repeater, and was experiencing a completely new depth of perception. Maybe the kid was looking through a window in time, or maybe stepping over on to a parallel wave, field, warp or whatever? McKinnon decided to have a talk with Leidermann before he left the island to get some idea of what might have happened. There were possibilities, he saw, in that if someone could look that far back — even if the whole episode was a dream passed down from mother to unborn child — yeah, that was it! Why not? It seemed a sensible argument when you thought about it. An unbroken memory stored in the brain and released by a surge of power. Hell, man's lineage was unbroken from his first step on the planet. Blood into blood. Links from the mindcells of the mother to the mindcells of the foetus. If that were true, he thought, you could look for the positions of tribes — Stone Age tribes — then dig up the remains. He would certainly have to have a word with Leidermann.

The skipboat paddled itself in an ungainly, turtle-like fashion up the ramp at Kyrenia and McKinnon took a taxi to the harbour hotel, deeply immersed in his thoughts. He left the taxi and walked through the front arc lights to the garden bar at the side of the hotel. Instinctively he looked towards the second table from the rear door and saw that he was still there, his bulk filling the basket chair, the hat back on the crown of his head, Canadian farmer-boy style.

"Hope the bastard bugs in that chair bite the ass off him," he muttered.

Suddenly he stopped and stared, and then, shaking a little, but determined, he walked across to the man who kept his eyes averted from the approaching McKinnon.

"Got a light?" asked McKinnon, reaching for a cigar from the hotel's courtesy box on the table.

"Please?" he added, his voice wavering along with his determination.

The big heavy-boned face turned slowly below him, expressionless, and the eyes looked coldly, disinterestedly, into McKinnon's. There was no movement of the hands of red leather and the legs still stretched forward, relaxed and crossed at the ankles.

"*Qué?*" said the large-lipped mouth.

McKinnon stared for a moment, then walked away, his legs boneless and quivering.

"Those lice," he muttered to himself, "they can't even use Canadians to do their leg-breaking – they have to use Xens." But who was he kidding? This time it was no femur job. It was his *neck*. They didn't send a man halfway across the world just to administer a fracture or two – and it *was* a hell of a lot of money.

He noticed he had crushed the end of the cigar and he threw it away in disgust. He did not smoke anyway.

And the cards? What hope did he stand of talking his way out of this one (maybe with a bribe) if the other guy didn't even understand his language. No hope at all. Zero.

"Get me a drink!" McKinnon shouted, startling the waiters with their glass-laden trays and causing one old man involuntarily to kick the underside of a garden table with his knee, thereby dislodging several other half-full glasses.

The trouble was, he mused, once he had a good stiff whisky inside him, the *Company* never forgave you once you crossed it. They may have let him out on a long leash if he had not skipped with a bundle when he was a cash-runner between states. They had broken both his legs that time – and warned him of worse should he cross them again.

Now it was a few dozen punters' markers – all of them belonging to the Company Officials, mobsters. He had *borrowed* against the markers, and lost. Now they wanted value for money, one way or another.

8

Contrary to Richard's expectations Esk did not cause him to suffer a lunatic outburst of mind-screaming when the caveboy woke in a different world to his Pleistocene home. He stayed back, it was true, almost out of reach, but he was quietly curious and a little stunned by his surroundings.

Richard unkindly subjected Esk to an onslaught of twentieth-century wonders by ordering a visiphone and dialling three hours of programmes. Then, as Richard exhausted himself and fell asleep, Esk removed their minds back to his own body in the hole beneath the tree away from the magical "Other World".

One reason Esk had not gone berserk on finding himself in the Other World was that he only partly believed in its existence as a tangible place. Dreams could be strangely real, especially after eating certain berries or leaves. Fantasy might have the substance of reality but Esk always awoke in the same bed in which he had lain the previous night. Dreams to a caveboy were only the other half of reality — a less distinct and memorable half, but part of one's physical adventures nonetheless. He and his comrades spoke of dreams as live experiences. One thing was certain about dreams, real or not: you always returned unscathed.

There was another occupant in the hole. A spider as big as an outspread hand was crawling across Esk's folded legs. The caveboy thought it about time his cell had some light inside it and he placed his feet against the remains of the fawn and pushed hard. The warmth immediately dissipated and the cold air of the Great Ice Age rushed into the pit.

Esk scrambled out of the hole and into the cool light of the fire-eye that had been split into narrow bars by the tree-tops.

The Mother had given him rebirth. He breathed deeply, making his lungs hurt, and then bent down to examine the carcass. Much of it was still intact and Esk could still go down to the camp in triumph! He did a little jig around the mutilated meat, crowing softly to himself about his hunting feat. Like most adolescents, half-man and half-boy, Esk acted like an adult for much of the time. Then it all became a bit too much for him and he had to do something crazy – shout and yell idiotic noises or jump up-and-down flapping his arms – for no sensible reason. Being an adult was an exhausting business and he had to open the safety valve occasionally. Next the boy quenched his thirst with some snow and ate a little of the raw meat. Then, heaving the deer onto his shoulders once again, and keeping a wary eye open for the panther, Esk began to make his way back to the path. Before he had gone very far Esk could detect the scent of people and he quickened his pace. Now that morning had come Granla would have sent out search parties.

A smallish creature ran across Esk's path.

It is possible that Richard might not have recognized the animal as a hare although it was a close forebear of that member of the *lagomorpha* family, and had the characteristic front incisors and strong hind legs.

Esk paused as the creature ran straight for his legs, swerved at the last moment and disappeared into the bushes at his back.

Something was out of phase with the rightness of the Mother's rhythms. Esk had recognized the animal by the white flash on its nose and he knew it to be one of the camp-fire hares. There were three – leverets taken from a snared mother – which had escaped to freedom later in life. All three, however, still came near to the camp to either play with the children in a game of no-touch tag, or for scraps of food. All three knew Esk as a harmless human and would have stopped near him – unless they were frightened of something.

The panther! Had it returned?

Esk stayed rigidly immobile and listened. The scent of humans was still on the air. More specifically, it was the smell

113

of Reng and two or three others Esk could name. This was one search party Esk would like to have avoided, for they were all cronies of his half-brother.

Why had the hare run from them? It knew Reng as well as Esk. The answer was simple. Humans do not change the way they look but when their mood alters they smell differently, act differently and sound differently. Therefore these aspects of the approaching group had not only been abnormal, but frighteningly so. The hare could smell either fear or blood-lust in the sweat of the group and Esk had a good idea which of those it was.

They had come to hunt him! To kill him if they found him alive, and dispose of his remains. After a night in the open the story of his death in the jaws of beasts would be readily believed. The Lundren would be blamed or any of the earth and stone creatures of the night, if not a bear or wolf pack.

The adrenalin surging through the body woke Richard.

What's wrong?

We are about to be butchered, Esk replied, just as a twig cracked in the trees ahead. Reng *was* the tribe's most brilliant tracker, after all.

"I see him!" came the shout. Then the sound of running feet.

This time the fawn was dropped and Esk took to this heels, snow patches disintegrated as he scattered their contents. A spear with a long point of edge-worked chalcedony flowed blue and brown past the corner of his eye. Reng's spear.

Esk ran with his heart pumping hard. He could hear the swift footsteps behind him as the animal-skin shoes, on those that wore them, slapped stone and damp logs. The trees began to move into his path as his chest constricted in the cold air causing him pain. Malicious trees. Why did they always impede the prey, never the predator?

Esk stumbled, badly cutting his skin, but he kept on running, building up a steady rhythm which carried him out of the steep treed slopes and onto the lime-thick descent to the cliffs.

Whop, whop, whop. The heart smacked inside his chest, easier now that it was a straight run. He took long strides, reaching forward with his toes, as he did when chasing the shore birds that had given him his name. ("*Esk! Esk! Esk!*"they had screeched as they ran on their stilt-long legs in the shallow water to get enough speed for take-off — before the caveboy's javelin pinned them to the claw-sucking sand.)

"Esk! Esk!" came the shouts of triumph from behind him and he glanced back quickly, giving Richard a glimpse of the pursuers too.

Why are you running? These are your people.

I know who they are and they've nearly caught me. They're my enemies. I'm the chosen one. They're the rivals. Are you stupid?

They *had* nearly caught him for they were only, in Richard's estimation, a hundred yards behind him. Thirteen seconds for a good boy runner to be up alongside! For a split second Richard took over the body, but lost speed. Running was not his forte. He retired again.

The chase began in earnest along the cliffs. Unfortunately the youths had cut Esk's path back to the rock shelter and he was now running in the opposite direction. There were still three youths in pursuit and Esk knew that if he stopped to draw breath he would be beaten to death.

They clung to his tail, determined this time not to be thwarted. He was Reng's prey and his half-brother wanted him badly. Richard was in an early time when strong blood ties and a sense of brotherly love were still to be formulated as wise family policy. Reng's world was a cave fronted by a semicircle of sea and with a hinterland of woods and mountains. He had seen waterspouts, tornadoes, violent storms full of white fire-spears and terrifyingly noisy balls of molten sky — but these were all things from the outside. These were the Mother's agents sent to punish, not to teach. Who had ever said, "Thou shalt not kill . . .?"

In Reng's world you killed *if* and *when* it became necessary, and it was necessary to Reng that Esk should die as soon as possible, brother or not.

He was cornered at the edge of a cliff some thirty feet high.

Below, the sea licked at the soft rock, placid enough but full of hidden dangers. No one could survive the sea. Esk awaited the stone that would cleave his breast. His heart beat more softly now. Reng moved in slowly since there was no escape. The stone axe was raised when Richard came to the fore.

Astounded, the three attackers watched as their quarry suddenly executed a near-perfect backdive from the edge of the cliff and entered the water, as clean as a long missile, below them. The youths were stricken with a wave of fear. The supernatural was at work. No one fell from a cliff so smoothly, so gracefully, as Esk had just done. No one hit the water from that height without making an enormous splash. "He has magic," said the one called Leaf, in awe.

Reng retorted, "He has just killed himself. He has no magic." But his voice lost its conviction towards the end of the sentence as they saw Esk's body come to the surface and begin moving swiftly across the top of the water.

Reng's complexion became pale.

"I have known him from birth," he said in a perplexed voice. "He was nothing special. Why should the Mother pick that little runt?"

The other two had been moving away from him as he spoke, anxious to be out of the proximity of the rival of the Mother's favourite. It seemed they wanted nothing to do with an opponent of a proven sorcerer.

"What's the matter with you?" growled Reng, realizing what they were doing. "I can still break both of you – don't desert me now."

"It's time we got back to the shelter," said Leaf, by way of reply. "The others will have reached there by now. The elders will be worried."

"Idiots," Reng snorted, brushing between the two youths and striding for the trees. They followed behind, at a safe distance, and Reng saw them exchange shame-faced glances.

Esk's body was being intimate with the sea mother and he did not like it. He passed an urgent thought forward. YOU FOOL — WE SHALL BE EATEN BY THE AGRIL!

There is no such thing.

But then Richard recalled seeing a drawing of an ichthyosaurus: long, narrow rods of teeth — like two jointed blade saws. He knew this was not the era in which these creatures appeared but there must have been sharks which were equally as unpleasant. His body tingled with alarm and he struck out for the shore, giving Esk, who had come forward to participate in the unusual sensation of running on his belly through water, a taste of speed.

Stim, thought Richard, the panic having now been transferred to him, *the sea must be teeming with razor-jawed, brainless creatures.* How long before one severed his leg or tore open his abdomen to let his intestines trail like ribbon in the water?

He made the shore without being eaten but the terror and lack of sleep had exhausted his mind. Almost immediately his thought processes dropped out of synchronization with the body and he fell into a deep sleep.

Esk, the thrill of wave-skimming over, began to assess his position. He was a long way from being safe. He decided that the best method of returning to the camp was to visit the Cave of Paintings and there to wait upon Granla — who would be sure to go there to record the hunt. That way the two of them could meet and Esk would have an escort back to the shelter.

No one can stop me now, he thought, his mind running over the events of the morning. I *am* magic. I *will* be Shaman.

He set forth for the Cave of Paintings.

The sun fired its rays indiscriminately over the prone bodies on Six Mile Beach, burning the skin that protected the flesh beneath. In the case of Leidermann, McKinnon noticed, the body covering was loose, folded in places, and of a strange mottled pattern. Some hides could be really ugly, he mused, remembering some of the beautiful white and black smooth-textured skins he had had his hands on at one time or another. He glanced down at his own bronzed, muscled body and hoped it would never turn into a Leidermann-type garment.

Adjusting his sunstrip — a semicircle of translucent polar-plane plastic to protect his eyes from the glare — he sat down beside the American on the sand.

Leidermann appeared to become aware of his sudden lack of sunshine and hoisted himself on to his elbow to look quizzically at his new neighbour on the beach. Sand stuck to the sweaty parts of his body, giving it a dead-fish appearance.

"Are you going to kick sand in my face?" asked Leidermann.

"What?" said McKinnon, taken off his guard.

Leidermann shook his head. "Nothing. You're probably not old enough to remember it. You American?"

"Canadian."

"Well, don't they have a lot of room in Canada?"

McKinnon said, "I don't know what you're talking about, mister, but yes, they do." His patriotism was stung.

"Then why're you crowding me, fellah? You've got the whole beach."

McKinnon laughed. "I see, yeah. Well, I came to talk to you. My name's McKinnon — I know Levan and his kid. The boy that had the accident?"

Leidermann sat up now and regarded McKinnon thoughtfully.

"I see," he said, parroting McKinnon.

"Look," replied McKinnon, attempting to clear up any preconceived misunderstandings. "I don't care about Levan and his kid. I just want to talk about what happened. I'm interested, see? I want to know how it was done."

"Why?"

"Because — look, I'll level with you. The boy thinks he's been on a time-trip — back to the Paleolithic era."

Leidermann squinted. "And you *believe* him?"

Cautiously McKinnon replied, "Not necessarily, but there might be something in it. Can't just dismiss it just like that — there are more things in heaven and earth . . ."

"Okay, okay," interrupted the professor. "What do you want from me? It's no good, I warn you, asking a lot of technical questions. Levan will tell you that. My title was bestowed, not earned. I'm a salesman, not a scientist."

A brown girl bounced by them and the attention of both men was distracted for a second.

"I see you're a man after my own tastes, Leidermann," said McKinnon, his respect for the bewhiskered, ageing American having fallen in the last few moments. The guy was nothing but a lecher with an expansive personality. Not a formidable intellectual.

"The reason I'm here is because of that," said McKinnon.

"Because of what? What are you trying to say?"

"Because of women — and other things like that. They cost money. Money isn't hard to find if you know where to look. If, say, we were to look somewhere and find a pack of Paleolithic skeletons."

"You're crazy. Where?"

"I don't know yet, but if one of us were to have the same sort of accident as the kid — stage a repeat — then we might be able to look into the past as he says that he can. See where the bastards bury each other. First-hand knowledge. Then we go find the spot and dig 'em up. Get it?"

Leidermann stared for a long time at the eyes behind the sunstrip, trying to gauge the depth of the lunacy that lay beneath them.

"You're crazy," he said at length. "Stark raving mad. Anyone who tried that trick would be killed stone dead."

"Richard Levan wasn't."

"Richard Levan was lucky," said Leidermann.

"Lucky enough to be still alive," the Canadian replied. He leaned back and settled his body on the sand. Nearby, church-bells began to toll. It was Sunday and the beach people shuffled guiltily in their sand-hollows hoping that God wouldn't notice them amongst a crowd. Somewhere in the foothills above, a half-witted youth was keeping time with the bells by donging the large empty waterjars that hung on either side of his donkey and as he rode he yelled a continuous stream of abuse at the unfortunate beast. It was, however, used to such treatment and in a way deserved it since it had been the donkey's kick that was responsible for the boy's addled brain.

In a bush nearby a spider, well out of reach of the Salamanders, had just completed a web – the result of several hours painstaking work – when a small finch flew through the lacework of threads, destroying it.

Without pausing the spider began again.

Later that day Leidermann received a visiphone call from Levan. The American had just completed his daily exercises on his hotel room floor.

"It's Richard," said Levan despairingly. "He's back into the same state as before."

"Ah," replied Leidermann unhelpfully. He wiped some dewdrops of sweat from his beard before replying. "Well, it's obviously one of those fluctuating illnessess. You can't expect him to recover completely just like that. He'll come round again – I promise you that."

Levan's face filled the screen, dark and ominous, as he leaned forward.

"Do you know something more than you've told me?"

"Only what the boy told you. About his mind being back in the Pleistocene era . . ." The thoughts crackled through Leidermann's mind as he spoke the words.

"Come on, Leidermann – this is real life, not a fairy story."

Dull. A dull, stupid reply.

Leidermann shook his head. "Okay, okay. But supposing – just supposing – the kid was telling the truth . . ."

"He is – he just . . ." began Levan angrily.

"Easy Levan, easy. Look, why do you think I'm still on the island? I'll tell you – because I *do* believe Richard. So do one or two other people I've talked to. . . ."

"McKinnon," said Levan scathingly.

"Not McKinnon. Others. This hasn't been the first accident of its kind."

"You *have* been keeping something back," shouted the enraged Levan, looking as if he would crawl through the screen if he could and strangle Leidermann.

"I've only heard *since*," the American shouted back. They stared dislike at one another.

The atmosphere was tense for a few moments, then Levan said, "All right, I believe you. Find out what you can for me. I'll . . . I'll pay you."

"Don't you ever think of anything but money?" sighed Leidermann. "Look, all I know is the same sort of accident happened to a woman in Sweden. She claimed she was having weird dreams about the Greeks – the Ancient Greeks, that is."

Levan seemed to read the American's expression and nodded, "And she's in a mental hospital, right?"

"Yes, but you know what the Swedes are like. No imagination." Dull, like you, he thought.

"I don't know what the Swedes are like," answered Levan in an even tone, "and I don't want to. I just want my son's mind to be returned to normal – Look. Let's play games then," he continued in a resigned voice, "though I honestly think you're halfway to the lunatic asylum yourself. What if my son is back in the days of the Ice Age – mentally – and something happens to the body he's inhabiting? What then?"

"I don't know."

"What *do* you know?"

"I think he'll be okay. This woman, the Swede. When the body she was inside – which was male, incidentally – was killed, she returned normal. Only thing was she stuck to her story, so they wouldn't let her out."

Levan was obviously trying to grasp a little of the unreality that Leidermann was attempting to push across to him. *Reach for it man*, thought Leidermann.

"What about the other side of this thing?" asked Levan. "What happens if Richard injures, or accidentally kills someone – they were violent times. Surely the lineage that person might have established throughout history will disappear? You know what I mean – stories have been written around it. Tread on a Mesozoic butterfly and change the future of the world. . . ." This was better.

"I have never subscribed to that theory," said Leidermann primly and firmly.

"What?" Levan shrank back from the screen, then added, "but what else is there? I mean – are there other theories?"

"Certainly there are. The one I personally accept is that *time* is an entity and as such exists in the ever *now* – which is why I believe your son may have crossed into the past. Why not, if all the seconds throughout history exist side-by-side?"

Levan shook his head as if he had something that he wanted to flick from it.

"Let's get this straight – Richard is still here, now, but he's in the past."

"Exactly – you grasp things quickly, Levan," Leidermann replied. "Look, think of it as an enormous circle – a circle of years turning in infinite space . . ."

"Around a traveller," added Levan, with more than a trace of sarcasm, which Leidermann duly ignored.

Leidermann continued, "To answer your first question, I believe in the *failsafe theory*. Let me explain. Since we're all here, all existing at the same time only occupying a different part of space – mankind throughout history – then nothing can change what already *is*. You say Richard might kill a man, say the night before that man should sire a son who would, in turn, produce offspring, etcetera, etcetera, until today, right?"

"Right."

"*Wrong*, Mr Levan. Even supposing the lineage of caveman were to continue uninterrupted – I mean, the son might die at birth, infant mortality rate being what it was in those times – there would be nothing to stop some other man siring that same son. Say caveman X produced three children and might reasonably have been expected to produce three more that lived. The nights he would have lain with his woman some other man would have been there instead. A widow doesn't have to remain celibate and a man can sleep with more women than one – in fact it's *likely* that she'll find another man. Don't you agree?"

"Yes, but . . ."

"No, no buts. If she's a clean, healthy woman she'll produce again, widow or not."

Levan snapped, "It's full of holes. What if the woman dies as a result of the man being killed? What about genes?"

"Development is only partially genetic – environment plays a major part too. We're talking about the Stone Age – cousins mating with cousins. The link will be replaced with a close substitute.

"Someone else will produce the child – don't you see, man, it's a *balance* and any single missing piece is going to be replaced, either by a barren woman becoming suddenly fertile or some other method. Given the limits of the resources, given the space and all the other necessities of life, breeding – of animals or men in natural conditions – will keep itself to those limits. If the unit becomes too large, the females are born infertile, if half the unit is wiped out the females will produce the offspring to fill the gap," he gestured with his hands. "This is all very general and I can see I'm having trouble convincing you, but that's the basis of the theory – balance. Biological failsafe mechanisms operate to maintain that balance. If a chance rockfall – or a careless time traveller – is responsible for a life, then that life will be replaced in one way or another."

He paused for breath and to see if he was having any effect. He always enjoyed this argument. Then he surged ahead.

"Good God, think of the implications of *your* theory. A single seed, from a single plant, would make a difference to history, if it were not in the last place the dying bird looked before flying into the jaws of the starving wolf that fed Romulus and Remus. . . . All the world balanced on a tiny seed drifting in the wind? Never. That's leaving everything to infinite chance, Mr Levan. I don't believe that we appeared, along with the rest of our necessities, fortuitously. There must be *some* order to the universe. It doesn't just happen. My God, have you any idea what the chances are of this world being exactly the right distance from the sun so as not to freeze or burn to a cinder, but to produce the atmosphere conducive to life as we know it?"

The barrage of words was obviously overwhelming Levan.

"No," he croaked.

"They are, to re-use an already well-used word, infinite. That's not pure chance, Levan," he continued, dropping the *Mr* once again. "That sort of situation requires a little order — and it's only one facet of our history. The *failsafe theory* means that if a single man — or group of men or women — are taken out of the string, then their individual actions, if essential to the flow, are compensated for by replacement. It's a simple theory but of course it's unpopular because it tends to injure the ego. We like to think we're essential to the running of things. A man doesn't like to think his particular discovery or invention — which may indeed have changed the course of history — would have been the product of another man had he not lived to the moment of conception. It happens all the time — a duplication of ideas across the world. Nobel Prize winners have arrived independently of one another at the same point of discovery at the same time. If the world is ready for it, then it will happen."

Levan stared at him for a long time, then suddenly, without another word he switched off, and the screen went blank.

"No imagination," sighed Leidermann, shaking his head.

The trees grew thicker around him as he walked. He had filled his belly with fruit and stone-ground rootmeal. One or two molluscs had had their shells cracked open and went on a final, speedy journey down the caveboy's dark oesophagus. Most of the time Esk liked the trees but he had just passed a bad thing — an omen — he thought. It had been one snake eating another snake and the scene, which he had difficulty in recognizing at first in the darkness of the trees, was grotesque enough to shock him; the piece of tail waving like a long thickly swollen tongue out of the mouth of the one that was eating.

He moved stealthily, afraid that his brother might have followed.

It was because he was moving so quietly that he heard the

voices from a long way off. Then came the scents – unfamiliar smells. He knew what it was. The other group that had invaded the land of the Gren – the short people with the large hands. Like ugly dwarves, the runner Nec-Nec had said.

Esk approached the cave slowly, from down-wind to avoid his scent from penetrating the camp, although there was such a lot of activity, and a huge fire with meat roasting, that the occupants of the camp would hardly have noticed an alien smell. Nevertheless Esk rolled his body in the cold damp earth and wet leaves of the undergrowth to camouflage the odour of sweat. He stung himself on nettles, which irritated him, but he accepted the pain as one of the hazards of crawling close to the Mother. She was chastising him gently for his misdeeds. He must learn to be more attentive to Her. She had never yet let him down.

The hubbub in the camp was painful to the caveboy's ears but he was as curious as any animal to see what was happening. There were more people than Esk had imagined and they were not as bent and hunched as Nec-Nec had described. Perhaps he had seen them only from a distance. These new people wore bearskins, not deerskin, which made them look even larger, and their weapons somehow seemed chunkier and less refined than those of Esk's group. Their voices were guttural and vulgar and the wide, toothy mouths gave their faces a devilish appearance.

Granla won't like this, thought Esk. The newcomers were defiling the Cave of Paintings. This was a holy place and their impiety and irreverence would not be tolerated by Granla or the Mother. Somebody would be hurt before long.

Esk stared through the leaves, drinking in the unholy spectacle of the ugly people stamping around the Cave of Paintings, when he saw his Shaman, trussed like a boar at a feast, being dragged by his heels into the cave. Esk's racing blood made Richard stir in his sleep.

The cave had a side entrance known to Esk and he decided the only way he was going to get back into his own camp alive was to take his Shaman with him. Besides, Esk was not yet tall and strong enough to take over in the role of leader. He needed Granla alive.

Making his way, still to windward, around the trees on the periphery of the newcomers' camp Esk found the cliff edge and began to sneak along. His movements took him near two old women who were scraping a skin. Their breasts hung like shrivelled thongs down to their waists and there was a fine, downy hair on their shoulders. Esk held his breath as he slid past them, timing his actions to coincide with the sound of the flint scrapers. The women kept up a constant skittering of conversation, almost as if they were talking to themselves rather than their companion, and neither paused to listen to what the other was saying.

Finding the boy-sized hole behind tall grasses, Esk crawled in and immediately felt the closeness of the Mother all around him, protective and reassuring. On all fours he crawled through the darkness of Her tunnels, further down into Her body until he could feel the stickiness of Her juices on his hands and knees, and the musty smell of Her flesh filled his head.

As he reached the end of the tunnel it opened out into a cavern. This was the secondary cavern, beyond the paintings. Esk kept well to the right because he knew that in the centre was a pit which dropped to the stomach of the Mother. He found the opening to the primary cavern and crawled the eight yards until he came out the other side – in the light.

The dwarves had arranged reed torches around the cavern which gave off a thick, foul-smelling smoke. Fortunately most of the smoke clung to the roof but even down below the atmosphere was heavy. Esk stared around the walls at the paintings which never failed to give him a thrill. Successive Shamans had produced these wonderful scenes of hunters and animals, and fish, too, with their simple colourful lines. The deer were especially beautiful, their antlers like trees and startled expressions on their faces. Hunters. Reng was there. (He had once tracked a spear-toothed monster and helped kill it in a pit. Everyone had feasted for a week on the beast's delicious entrails.) So too was Esk's uncle, being attacked and killed by a pack of dholes. (He had tried to steal their kill.)

Esk was not there but his younger brother Slek was there, a stick-boy playing his reed flute. The group loved Slek for the tunes he stole from the Mother and blew through the holes in his flute. It was a talent which helped him avoid more onerous tasks, such as skinning, or making burins out of flint blocks.

So busy was the boy in studying the fruit of his own people he did not notice one of the squatters approach him until he felt himself being lifted off his feet by strong arms. He stared into an ugly-looking face and then shrieked when a tongue appeared through the beard on the side of it and waggled at him.

The newcomer's arms were as strong as trees and he laughed in delight when he saw how he had terrified the boy. Heaving Esk on to his shoulders he stumbled his way over the slippery cavern floor and eventually out into the light of the day. The fire-eye will turn and I shall not see its full cycle this time, thought Esk.

They crowded round him and poked at his red skin, making animal-like noises in their throats. One of the children pushed a finger maliciously into his eye, making it water, while another bit savagely at his toe. Richard woke and felt the terror. Looking out he saw a nightmare of faces and knew them immediately for Neanderthals, having seen their pictures many times in his father's books.

Get away from these people, he foolishly warned Esk.

Take us to that other place, responded Esk. Richard almost obliged and then remembered that Esk's body would merely crumple where it stood. The crowd of Neanderthals would probably toss the body somewhere and being none too gentle creatures might break a limb or two. It was best to wait until it was time to sleep for Richard had to occupy the body too and it would not be pleasant having to keep well back to avoid the pain of a fracture.

The ordeal of running the gauntlet was over when an aggressive, monkey-faced individual who was obviously the leader ordered the other Neanderthals about their various businesses and took Esk by the hair. Grinning into his face for a second he then thrust the youth towards a female who was ugly, even for her own kind. The woman was stronger than the boy and dragged him into the trees where Esk had been hiding just a short time before. Her brutish lips glistened with spittle as she ripped away her garment and then tore at Esk's shorts.

What's she doing? screamed Richard silently, terrified of the thought of what he knew was happening. Esk's reply was distorted, for he too was almost beside himself with terror.

The girl bit him on the shoulder viciously and he whimpered. Richard came through, as Esk surrendered and seized a stone. He swung it at the female head that rocked and dipped from the sky above, intending to smash the temple. The stone never arrived.

9

Richard loved mountains. He liked to approach them in a slider from a long way off and watch them grow before his eyes to breathtaking giants. He liked to travel the winding road of Olympus through a tapestry of agricultural scenes, from the vineyards of the lower terraces to the cherry and apple orchards near to the top. It was a pity Esk was asleep and missing it all.

The slider hummed by drystone walls on its route, brushing the wild flowers of the mountain's skirts; past monasteries teetering on aggressive chins of rock; beneath the boughs of Stone pines; into stole-white mists draped around the head of the dowager. This was his mountain, Olympus, and he loved it. He was managing to expel thoughts of the nightmare encounter with the Neanderthal woman.

"Want to stop for some apples?" he asked McKinnon. It was traditional and although it was McKinnon's hired slider in which he was riding he felt it his duty to make the offer, since Rosemary's father was a visitor, not a resident of Cyprus.

"Er, no thanks," replied McKinnon, who appeared to be engrossed with his driving.

"Chrome," said Richard, pointing to a white scar on the flank of the Troodos hills below them.

"What's that kid?"

"Chrome mines – closed now. Down there. There's copper, too, in other places. Did you know the name of Cyprus is supposed to come from the word copper?"

"Or *kypros*, which is the Ancient Greek word for henna," replied McKinnon.

Richard blinked, "How did you know that?" he asked.

"Think I'm stupid because I'm supposed to be irresponsible?" said McKinnon smiling. "I got it from a visiphone guide programme," he added, as a feeling of embarrassment grew within Richard.

"Sorry," said Richard.

"Okay."

They travelled on towards the peak in silence. McKinnon had arrived at about two o'clock in the afternoon, in Richard's room at the hospital, shortly after Richard's father had left, and suggested that the two of them go for a drive. Richard was bored and saw no reason why he shouldn't go with McKinnon, with whom he'd talked previously at Loraine's request, although he was fairly sure that no one else was aware of the plan. McKinnon was one of those men in whom adolescents instinctively place their trust. Owning a naturally easy, uninhibited manner coupled with a genuine fondness for everything youthful, McKinnon didn't find it difficult to converse with young people on their own level. He took an interest in teenage trends and could use the current catchphrases. And he could also develop interests and passionate enthusiasms overnight.

"What about the doctor?" Richard had asked.

McKinnon replied, "Oh . . . he won't mind. A bit of fresh air will do you good. I'll get you back in time for dinner tonight."

As Richard was dressing in the clothes McKinnon had brought for him the man asked, "What did your father have to say? Today, I mean. About your relapse."

Richard frowned. "He was anxious, I suppose. Happy that I . . . that I'm in my right mind '*once again*' as he put it, but now he's gone to phone someone in Sweden. Another doctor."

"I see," murmured McKinnon. "Is he coming back?"

"Not till this evening. Look, Mr McKinnon, why do you want to take me to Troodos — to the mountains?" Richard was beginning to suspect an ulterior motive behind McKinnon's desire to "get to know him better". McKinnon had looked at Richard for a long time before saying, "Call me Alan. Thing is, I'm in pretty hot water. Some guy's going to hurt me very badly unless I can produce some money I owe him — which I don't have. I figure if your story is true then you may be able to lead us to a Paleolithic burial site. We'll split the proceeds – fifty-fifty. What do you think, kid? A good idea?"

"Then you believe my story – about the time travel?" Richard was putting the Canadian to the acid test. Even Rosemary had failed this one. McKinnon turned out to be no exception.

"Not necessarily, but I believe your mind may be re-creating something of the past while you lie in your bed. Look, tell me something, Rick – when you leave your caveboy's body, is it the same time of day here? I mean, when your mind zooms back to the present it may be midday to your caveboy – is it noon when you wake up in your own body?"

Richard answered defensively, "No, but it doesn't prove a thing. I left the other body at about three in the afternoon and opened my eyes about ten o'clock in the morning here – but I've thought about that. At least two explanations are pretty obvious to anyone. Firstly, the speed of the Earth's rotation has probably changed – slowed or quickened – so if the changeover is instantaneous then it may be that daytime has altered. If not, I'd have thought it would take time to travel through time. I mean, it may take some hours of real time for the two minds to move over thirty or so thousand years. . . ."

"Let me speak to this caveboy," said McKinnon quickly.

Richard was annoyed enough to be outspoken. "Look, Mr McKinnon, my friend's here, in the back of my mind. I can feel him." He didn't feel as inhibited with Alan McKinnon as he did with his own father. His father was too distant, too aware of the proper responsibility of a father towards his son. Richard was always afraid he might displease his father, whereas he was fairly certain it would take a lot from him to gain McKinnon's disapproval. Anyway, it didn't matter if McKinnon felt displeasure. He meant nothing to Richard.

"I don't doubt you *feel* him, Rick. That doesn't mean he's real."

"He's asleep and I can't wake him up. I wouldn't, anyway, just to satisfy you. I don't think I want to come for a ride now."

But eventually he changed his mind. McKinnon persuaded the reluctant Richard that he didn't think him mad but that the boy could not expect people to accept what appeared to be a supernatural experience, without offering any proof. Okay, okay, he had said. He didn't want the caveboy to come forward, but they might need him later if they couldn't find the place where the Neanderthals had lived.

So the pair of them – or rather three of them – were gliding up the shoulder of Mount Olympus in search of the Cave of Paintings. On the way Richard recounted his experiences with the Cro-Magnons. Once they reached the top McKinnon parked the slider beneath a cypress tree and they had the island spread out below them like a pool of frozen malt.

"Okay," said McKinnon, the breeze lifting his hair, "where is it? Which direction?"

It was cool on the peak and Richard shivered involuntarily. He faltered. "I don't know," he said truthfully.

McKinnon put a friendly arm around his shoulder, which immediately made the boy feel uncomfortable. He didn't even like his father touching him.

"Okay, let's take this from the beginning. Over there, on the other side of the Kyrenia range, is where your father found the rock shelf. Now, where did you – in your other body – go to hunt the deer?"

Encouraged, Richard replied, "Straight up the mountains, through a pass." He shrugged the arm from his back. McKinnon grinned at the youth.

"Right then. That would put you on top of the range. . . ."

"No – we came down again before climbing once more. See, that high ground there!" Richard pointed excitedly. "That's probably where we found the herd."

McKinnon studied the map he had in his hand. "That's Karpasha. Okay. Now, when you started running away – after you got out of that hole. What then?"

Richard frowned. "We were both scared. It's difficult to remember. . . ."

"Think! Which way was the sun? In your eyes?"

"No, I don't think so," said Richard slowly. "Behind me, I think. Behind us, I mean."

"Him, you, it doesn't matter. So that leaves you running west, towards Morphou Bay. Is that where you dived in?"

"Well, we ran along the shoreline for some distance. Then when I had dived off the overhang we started heading inland – I fell asleep." McKinnon crumpled the map.

"Goddam," he said, savagely. Then, smoothing out the plastic again, he asked carefully, "How long did you run for? Along the shore?"

"I didn't have my watch on," replied Richard coolly. "Look, Mr McKinnon, I think we ought to go back if you're going to keep losing your temper."

"Forget my temper – try to guess. An hour? Half an hour?"

"Not as long as that, about twenty minutes. *I remember*, we were heading straight for the high Troodos range when we left the water. I mean – he – oh, it doesn't matter."

McKinnon's eyes began to show some hope.

"So that would put you down there – somewhere in that area amongst the foothills." He pointed down the mountain, north-northwestward.

"It could be. But that's a pretty big piece of ground."

"Never mind," replied the man. "We've got somewhere to begin looking. Perhaps when we get down there something will click. There can't be that many caves around ... we'll ask someone. A local should be able to put us on to any caves in the vicinity."

They climbed back into the slider and McKinnon drove down the far side of the Troodos range. Both occupants of the machine were excited at the prospect of finding the cave. If the paintings were still there, thought Richard, what a triumph that would be for his father. A rival for Lascaux or Teruel? He knew McKinnon was only interested in finding the skeletons, so perhaps the Canadian would allow Richard's father to reap the benefits of the cave itself?

On the slopes below they found various places to search, for there were many small spurs and ridges. Once they were threatened by a farmer with an ancient-looking weapon – a shotgun of sorts – because they had apparently trodden over some newly planted olive trees. McKinnon had to placate the man with a fistul of coins, even though the trees did not look at all worse for their walking through the fledglings grove. (McKinnon would have cuffed the farmer if Richard had not insisted they settle things quietly.)

Each time they found a new overhang the excitement surged through Richard's breast. But time after time the find yielded no cave. The optimism was high, however, and there were plenty of new places to search.

While they looked McKinnon told Richard tales of his youth. As the son of a lumberjack working the Canadian Shield, he grew up in a wild environment – one of the last refuges from urban civilization. His father was a member of a dying trade and though he had, in his time, hacked down the giants with an axe, technology kept progress with his experience until, by the time Alan was fourteen years of age, they were using mobile machines to cut through the forest.

The gamble. You *know* when you feel lucky and today McKinnon didn't feel lucky. That meant they wouldn't find the cave – so what was the point in looking? But his luck might change. He might get the *feeling*.

Finally, he said to Richard, "Don't you have *any* idea where you are? Hell, where's your *instinct*, boy?"

Richard, probably tired with scouring the countryside after being in bed for so long, seemed to withdraw into himself and took on a sullen expression.

"Well, answer me Richard." McKinnon was not going to let go easily, bad run of luck or not.

Richard replied, "*You* can't talk to me like that – you're not my father."

McKinnon grabbed his arm and wheeled him round to face him.

"You can thank God I'm not, boy, because if I was your ass would be as red as that sun."

"Go to hell."

McKinnon gritted his teeth in frustration.

134

"Goddam, I'm warning you."

The eyes glared back at him and then, quite suddenly, they changed. They became alert – and sly – and flicked from side to side.

A chilling pain stabbed McKinnon in his cheekbones, like an immediate attack of the sinusitis which he occasionally suffered.

"Goddam," he repeated, only this time the word came out slowly and was laden with something akin to fear.

The youth turned, looking with jerky movements over the range of foothills. Then, when he turned back again, the eyes had returned to normal.

"He's awake," said Richard. "I let him have a look but either we're in the wrong place or the landscape has changed."

McKinnon breathed out slowly, getting hold of his nerves.

"Don't use schoolboy tricks to impress me. Was that ... was that him? That ... looked at me like that?"

The sun was dropping and Richard's voice was reflecting his weariness.

"Yes, it was. If I drop out now – fall off to sleep – he'll take over. I don't want to do that because he might do something silly. He's not used to things as we know them."

"Don't you fall asleep," said McKinnon quickly. "You stay awake. I'll get you back to the hospital."

The eyes had been those of an animal. A vicious beast. The thing inside Richard could very well tear open his throat, like a savage wolf, if allowed free rein. The kid was a schizophrenic, just as Levan had feared. My God, thought McKinnon, I don't want to be locked up in my slider with a lunatic. It was not so much the boy but the madman inside that frightened him.

McKinnon tripped on a piece of rotten log as they walked down the slope towards the slider. Something stirred in the hollow left by the aerated wood and made him jump backwards. It was a coiled black snake some three feet in length. The reptile unwound and began side-winding away.

He began shaking, though more from the feverish excitement and rapid heartbeat generated by a dangerous situation

135

than fear. Taking two quick strides forward he stamped on the snake's head, crushing it. The black length twisted into knots of agony, the red, shapeless head staining the dust.

"Snake," he said, breathing quickly.

A noise made him look up sharply to see Richard staring at him, white-faced, with two sharp spots of colour on his cheeks.

"That snake was harmless," said Richard in a tight voice. "It also helps to keep the rats down."

"How the hell was I supposed to know that?"

"You could have asked. Instead you just kill it.'

"It might have bitten me," McKinnon said evenly, "and then it would be too late to ask, wouldn't it?"

"It was moving away from you – you just like killing things. I . . . I watched your face. You enjoyed it."

"Now that's not quite true . . . okay, I got excited, but I *did* think it was poisonous. It's a natural reaction. I can't walk around with an encyclopedia."

Richard mumbled something and moved towards the slider.

The slider whispered through an arch of Aleppo pines which formed a guard of honour on either side of the road. *Here comes the bride*, Richard hummed in his mind, *all fat and wide*. He was studying the cirrus cloud, veils of white painted on the reddening sky by a lazily wielded brush. Richard was gradually slipping into a state of detachment from the world. He and McKinnon had not spoken since the snake-killing incident and the silence and motion of the vehicle were sleep-inducing. Richard tried to keep his eyes open, however, because he knew that once he fell asleep, and Esk woke, the caveboy would slip naturally – or unnaturally – back to his own body, taking Richard with him.

I wonder if I *am* dreaming it all? thought Richard, as the slider reached the shore and began skimming along in the shallows. It didn't matter. It was real enough to him. He could feel Esk sleeping in his head, pressing close to his own mind. Too close really, for the caveboy had not fully withdrawn before going back to sleep and occasionally a thought flickered through his mind and Richard caught it too. Some of Esk's thoughts were strange and frightening.

Possibly McKinnon had the best answer. That Richard's mind was re-creating an historical event. Somehow he had become receptive to past happenings, like running a visiphone programme through his mind, using his eyes as the visual display unit. No, that wasn't right. Still, it was a more comforting theory than his father's: that Richard was halfway to the cabbage patch.

The sky was very red tonight.

He looked towards the cliffs, the place where an earthquake had once shaken cracks into the ground making it unsafe for walking. One or two cranes were still flying, the dying sunlight setting fire to their white feathers. Cyprus was a staging post for many different birds *en route* to the African coast from Europe and Asia Minor. The departure from the island of migratory buzzards to North Africa was always the same, as Richard had often witnessed. Day by day they arrived in a wide front on the north coast of the island and converged on the salt lake at Akrotiri. In the early hours – usually between eight o'clock in the morning and midday – one or two birds began circling the lake. These attracted others until, in less than ten minutes, a thousand buzzards were wheeling on thermals above the water. They rose higher and higher until, almost lost from sight, they moved south across Akrotiri and slowly out to sea.

The sky red.

A spot formed, by a piece of cirrus. A bird? Perhaps a late or lost buzzard? thought Richard. He watched it as it gradually grew, spreading out flimsy wings against the background of scarlet: wings, and a thin, boat-shaped body with waving antennae, dew-dropped with heavy crystals at their tips.

Stim! What was happening?

Patterns formed on the wings in fantastic colours. Turquoise and purple, angry blotches, one on each wing like Rorschach test cards. Silver rimmed the edges, and the central body grew darker with the cliffs. It was a butterfly, filling the world with its slow, lazy movements – the antennae curved, following the natural line of the Earth. It covered all horizons, menacing in its gossamer hugeness. An aerial archway was formed as the butterfly dragged its wings along the surface of the sea. Mount Olympus could have passed beneath without touching the harp of gauze.

The larger the shape grew the flimsier and more delicate became the wings, and the darker and more sinister was the ridged body. Rivers of veins formed, running like mercury through the giant, and fine hair appeared on the torso. The wings folded around the tiny craft. Richard moaned in the back of his throat. Please lord, please lord, please lord, let me wake up!

But he wasn't dreaming. McKinnon was still there beside him, asking him what was the matter? Why he was making that noise?

Holes began to appear in the wings, like tissue burned from beneath, the flame invisible. Quickly they became tattered and pieces floated down into the sea, hissing as they gently entered the waves.

The body of the gargantuan butterfly remained, transforming suddenly into a dragonfly and skimming the surface of the water with the sound of a dozen monorail engines, its slip-stream forcing a channel to appear in the sea. It maintained a course, directly adjacent to the slider, then inwards, towards them, as if attacking. At the last moment it turned upwards, flying over them. Richard ducked instinctively but not before he had seen the dragonfly's rider. It was the Neanderthal girl that had raped Esk, naked and screaming astride the first segment – in her hand was a spear of pink quartz.

Richard then realized what was happening. He was sharing Esk's dreams – or nightmares. The caveboy *was* too close. The images were filtering through into the reality of Richard's world.

The dragonfly made another low pass and this time Richard could clearly see the girl's appalling features – bulbous lips leering at the slider's occupants, eyes wide, the pupils glistening with passion.

Behind the girl came a spider, immense yet friable, tripping over the waves. Then standing, waiting for the slider to run beneath its archway of legs.

"Stop the slider," screamed Richard, reaching forward and turning the switch.

The vehicle slewed sideways as the motor cut, and entered the waves at an angle.

"You crazy . . ." began McKinnon, but then he cracked his head on the hatchway as the slider struck the sandy bottom of the ocean. It settled into the sand in about ten feet of water. The water entered the electrics and there was a noise akin to frying from the motor region as McKinnon tried to restart the vehicle.

McKinnon, his head bleeding from the blow it had taken, began reaching for the switch to open the hatch, his fingers like spiders themselves, scrambling in an agony of panic to escape death by suffocation. The electrics had gone. The hatch failed to open. He grabbed the manual lever.

"Leave it!" cried Richard sharply.

"You crazy? We'll drown," said McKinnon. "We have to get out." His eyes had left his mind behind.

The greenness swirled darkly around the cockpit of the slider – the greenness of old bottle glass, peppered with dancing air bubbles.

"You open that hatch we *will* drown," rapped Richard. "The water will come rushing in and force us downwards. We'll never get out."

The water in the interior had covered their ankles and the silence was deep.

Some sanity trickled into McKinnon's eyes. Some of the slackness disappeared from its features. The fingers stopped crawling.

"Yeah, I think you're right. We have some air. We aren't drowning right at this moment."

"If we stay here," said Richard, trying also to cope with the now awake and inquisitive Esk, "and let the slider fill slowly, when the water reaches to our necks we open the hatch and, after a couple of seconds, swim out."

"Can *you* swim?" asked McKinnon quickly.

Richard looked at the man quickly. No wonder he had panicked, going against every survival manual ever printed – or perhaps adults did not read them?

"Can't you swim?" he asked McKinnon.

We ride the water again? came Esk, catching the thought that accompanied the enquiry.

Richard confirmed the picture. He felt unafraid, always being at home in the water. If you followed the rules there was no chance of drowning. It was, after all, only shallow. Since Richard felt unafraid Esk had no cause to feel concern and was as complacent as a fish in a tank of its own.

McKinnon said, "Only just. I'll be able to flap my way back but if *you* couldn't swim there would have been no way I could have saved you."

"You might as well have stayed with me then because my father would have killed you."

"Don't get too smart," replied McKinnon. "It's ill-mannered and pig-ignorant." The water was up to their waists now.

Richard was suitably abashed. "Sorry," he said.

It was cold and as the waterline passed his nipples even Richard began to grow anxious – which in turn made Esk agitated.

"That hatch *will* work won't it?" he said, his teeth chattering with the chill atmosphere of the slider.

McKinnon seemed to be in full command of both his nerves and his faculties now.

"It'll open," he said. "If I have to do it with my teeth."

The water reached Richard's chin a thousand years later. He sat up, as high as he could, and a few moments after that McKinnon pulled the lever. Nothing happened. Then, the same thought must have occurred to McKinnon, simultaneously with that of Richard's. *The slider hatch opened outwards.* A few more moments and the cockpit was full, a push and a kick and

Richard was shooting upwards. He bobbed out, showering the star clusters with seawater. A moment later McKinnon had joined him and seemed to be reaching, clutching at the silver decorations overhead and gasping for breath.

"Here . . ." said Richard, grabbing for the man's collar.

Together they struggled towards the shore, Richard swimming sidestroke and McKinnon slapping the water with awkward, drunk-like arm movements. He had not been fooling when he said he was a poor swimmer, thought Richard.

They made the shallows, having both swallowed a fair proportion of the Mediterranean each, and staggered onto the beach to flop down and enjoy a few moments of retrieved existence. The banks of stars had moved away now, did not seem to be crowding them anymore. Somewhere in the hills behind them a cricket played a passionate tune on his sawtoothed violin. Or perhaps it was one of the other pibrochs which made up his total repertoire?

Inside Richard's head Esk was winning what was becoming a customary struggle. Finally the blackness began to descend. The last thing he heard was McKinnon saying, "Hang on, kid. Don't pass out on me – I'll hitch a lift for . . ."

"When I get my hands on him I'll kill that bastard!"

Levan stormed out of the air conditioned hospital into the balmy evening outside and glared belligerently at Loraine. He had just left Richard in his room.

"Don't tell me, tell him," she replied.

"Him?" fumed Levan. "He's gone back to the Troodos mountains – probably to some hotel where I can't reach him. What right did he have? Taking the boy away from the hospital in the first place? I don't mind if he kills himself, but he's not going to take my son with him."

Levan had a mental picture of the waves scything at the body of his son, trying to pare the body to the bone with their liquid blades. He shook the image away.

Loraine said, "Stop getting so heated – and pompous . . ."

"Pompous?" The word exploded.

"Yes, like that."

He took a deep breath, staring directly into her face. She was not being obstructive – he could see that in her eyes. She had that damp look in them. The one that meant she was being sympathetic.

"Okay," he replied gathering himself together mentally. "The boy's all right, physically – but he's had another relapse."

"The doctor told you that might happen for a while. So long as he keeps recovering . . ."

"So long as he does."

He was breathing more easily now. He no longer wanted to find McKinnon and smash his head to a bloody pulp with a brick. He would still like to push his fist into McKinnon's face but that wasn't murder – just plain schoolboy revenge.

"Whatever possessed him?" he said, still unable to understand the irresponsibility, the plain stupidity of McKinnon's action. People in Levan's world didn't behave like that. "I still can't believe it."

"I know," said Loraine. "You've told me a dozen times already."

He shook away the image and put his arm around Loraine. She looked prim, which was difficult for a woman who battled against a natural tendency to tartiness. A pink ribbon had been out of place in her hair from the age of fourteen.

"Okay, I've calmed down," he said.

"There's no reason why you should. It's just . . . oh, I don't know – why do we always have to fight, Paul?" She joined her hands around his neck and pressed a warm, soft cheek against his shoulder. The thin shirt did not form any sort of barrier at all against the heat she was generating. It had been some time since she had held him like that and if he could have pulled out the cord which supplied the world with its turning power, at that moment, he would have done so.

"Keep it up, I'm beginning to like it," he said.

The door to the hospital slid open and a woman wearing a white shawl over a silver evening gown passed by them, smiling vacantly: she hardly seemed to notice them. A visitor – or maybe a nurse with a heavy date? Some moments later he heard the sound of a slider hatch opening and he guessed it was a nurse because the staff slider ports were in that direction. She had been a slim girl, in the mould of Velasquez's *Venus*. The white sandals on her feet had been of thread-thin straps and the feet themselves dainty — Levan's hand would have swallowed one whole. He looked back at Loraine standing beside him. She was wearing a sun-faded blue and white striped sailing vest — her bosom, unsupported, hung heavy and low. Definitely Boucher's *Miss O'Murphy*.

But, dammit, he liked her that way.

10

The totem of the three skulls had been disassembled and lay in pieces at the feet of the two women, one a blind, old crone.

"What's happening now?" asked the blind one, in a voice not dissimilar from the scraping of a burin on sandstone. Her hair was a river of thick grease and as grey as the cloak of wolfskin she wore. Knots of fat and excrement gave both the living and the dead follicles a nobbled appearance. These decorations to her person proclaimed her status as a priestess.

"Skell has ordered the lighting of the fires," answered her daughter, "nothing else. Pay attention to your tasks, you barren old sow." She insulted her mother as a matter of course. The old woman had treated her badly when she was a child. Now her mother's eyes were lying somewhere on the snows of the north country – torn out in a clawing match with another female who had since deserted the group to become a woman of the Tall Ones.

Her spirit still unbroken the priestess replied, "I can still do things many others cannot. You should be good to your mother . . ." she grumbled as she deftly fitted the three skulls, one inside the other until the painted mastodon skull housed the human skull and inside the latter dangled the headbone of a mouse. Only the blind were permitted to touch the totem. Theirs was a holy office presided over by the Shaman himself. Any power they derived from that office was offset by their blindness and they were, therefore, no threat to the Shaman.

"Give me the wooden stake," the blind one rasped, her arthritic fingers fumbling over the ground in front of her, trying to find the prop for the skulls.

The daughter grinned spitefully showing a fence of broken

teeth, watching her mother's gnarled hands scrambling, like starving rats, completely in the wrong direction.

"Where is it? Where is it?" screeched the old woman after a while. One of the men called out: asking what was the matter.

The woman quickly directed her mother's fingers towards the carved stake. She would be beaten if she was caught tormenting the priestess. A hand grasped the painted wooden skulls of the prop and dragged it closer to fit the top end to the mastodon's jaw. Two of the mastodon's tusks lay nearby. These would help support the skulls' weight, the points being positioned in the eye sockets and the bases in the earth.

"The worshipping of the heads starts early tonight," said the daughter. "They wish to kill the stranger quickly. Skell wanted to keep him alive at first but the Tall One bit his neck when he leaned too close." She giggled nervously at the thought, then remembered her mother was only blind, not deaf.

"I'm laughing at the death of the stranger," she said quickly, unable to keep her voice free of a tremor of fear.

"Yes, yes," said the crone in a crafty tone of voice. "We all know how you like the Shaman. So I'm an old sow, eh? Fat female pig?"

"No, no. That was just my way," replied the daughter, fingering the scar which Skell had given her as a gift for refusing his advances one night. He had applied the edge of a hot stone to her belly, burning his own hand in the process, such had been his rage.

"*You* know my way, mother."

The crone's hand flashed out, grabbing her daughter's hair and pulling the other woman's face closer.

"He doesn't look at you now, though, does he child? Why? Because you are old and wrinkled like your mother. A lizard's skin hangs from your bones and your breasts like strings with small knots for nipples. Now you wish he would look at you, eh? Now you wish for a man to warm your thighs at night, be he the lustful greedy oaf the Shaman is, or not. Women grow old quickly — the fires drying the skin on their cheekbones, reddening their eyes, and the work and children pulling the soft

145

fat of their breasts down to their buttocks and hips. I know you were with the boy – the stranger – he failed you didn't he," she cackled, "like all the others. . . ."

"I hate you!" sobbed the daughter in pain and frustration, trying to prise open the fingers.

"When you're dead I'll throw your brains to the scavenging dogs – you'll live inside a bitch, you old bitch, and I'll use your skull for a . . . a . . ."

The priestess shrieked with laughter at the implied obscenity, flinging the other from her. They got on well together, mother and daughter. Life was never without interest.

Several of the woman dragged the unfortunate Shaman from his own damp hole and out under the night frosts. There were fires arranged in circles and behind these glinted white, eager-looking faces. Granla blinked, even in that poor light, for his eyes had been staring down into the blackness of a deep well since he had been caught and trussed by his captors.

They cut his bonds, allowing a free flow of blood into his cramped limbs and one of the women ground a heel into his face before retreating quickly behind the fires. His face was so numb the hurt did not touch him although he could feel the warm blood inside his mouth. He sat up, rubbed his scored wrists and ankles. The pain of the blood entering his extremities made him wince.

He was alone, inside the fires.

Granla was aware of the eyes upon him, and, finding himself beneath a gruesomely painted skull of a spear-tooth, knew that he was not going to escape the ring of fires with his life. Once this fact had settled in his intelligence, he faced his prospects calmly and with the sound heart that had always helped him maintain his position as Shaman of his people.

They were waiting for something – or someone – those faces that formed the immediate horizon. Was he supposed to offer a supplication to their god? They would wait forever!

He stood up and shook himself before deliberately projecting as large a globule of spittle as his dry mouth could muster, directly between the sockets of the huge skull before him. It dribbled down the crudely administered designs that offended his artistic eye so much, and he grinned. There was a moan from the faces. He realized he had succeeded in attacking their collective sensitivity.

Somewhere, out in the night, a wolf howled. Granla, about to die, joined the animal in its mournful rendering. The sound was full of sadness, filling the cave behind with its melancholy note. A second cry from Granla was drawn from the depths of early time and he dimly perceived a stirring amongst his antagonists. He was still the magic man.

Then the drums began: the slow beat upon hollow stones and logs, becoming faster, keeping pace with excited hearts.

Finally, when the drumming reached the point where the single beats were indistinguishable from one another and ran together, forming a continuous note, a shadow stretched in front of Granla. He looked to its owner, a heavily built individual that had stepped inside the ring of fires. Purposefully, the figure moved forward in a crouched stance and clearly Granla was meant to wrestle with this shorter but stockier representative of another branch of the family of Man. The face before him was dark and heavy, with two small bestial eyes shining from within their deep pits. Lank hair fell over the heavy forehead and sparse stubble covered the chin and cheeks. Bubbles were forming on one of those cheeks, like the balloons of skin that expanded under the throats of tree lizards. They made him want to pinch the tight spheres and watch them deflate. He would pinch this one's throat and block the tubular lifeline down which the Mother breathed Her sweet breath, he vowed silently.

No! He would not help these ugly people kill him quickly. They would know it was Granla with whom they dealt. Not some fool who fell into the hands of their tribe's best wrestler.

"Urghh!" Granla growled, working himself up into the state of frenzy which had never failed to quell his opponents before that night.

"Yahhr – arrh – agrr."

The aggressor paused in his tracks. Granla screamed, high, loud and incoherently, before snatching one of the tusks from beside the skull and driving its point hard into the chest of his adversary.

The strong one with the hole in his cheek wrenched the makeshift lance free from his chest. He growled deep in his throat. Blood seeped from his wound. Far from keeling over in death he merely looked faintly annoyed.

Granla began to feel the prickling of fear.

He took one step backwards as his aggressive opponent rushed forwards to grip his chest in powerful arms. He could feel the wetness. They stood like statues, fused to each other in the firelight. Granla could smell the strong odour of sweat from the other's armpits. He grasped the man's ears and attempted to twist the head. Hole-in-the-cheek squeezed. A loud crack sounded, followed by another, and another. Three of Granla's ribs were broken.

In pain and anger he let go of one of the ears and punched the thick throat, once, twice, thrice, again and again, until the arms around him began to weaken. He still held the ear with his left hand and the eyes in the other's face rolled into whiteness as Granla's strong fist slammed repeatedly into the vulnerable windpipe. Finally he struck Hole-in-the-cheek between the nose and the upper lip with all the force he could muster. The stocky body slipped from him.

Bending down, through the blinding pain in his chest, he found the second tusk. Lifting it he drove it downwards. The bubbles came again through the hole, accompanying the scream. This time they were red.

There was a silence as deep as the tunnel of time. Granla stood, tall and defiant in the firelight. Then they fell on him in droves, hacking with stone knives and axes. One man wailing a single sound impregnated with anguish.

"Craaaaak!"

To attack him with such venom, he must have hurt them. The granite man died happy.

Esk's feelings as he watched the death of his Shaman were a mixture of sadness and fear – fear for the group now that their great leader had gone. Certainly, there in the light of the night fires, he felt no wish to claim the position for himself. It was too soon. He was too young.

He shivered as he watched the newcomers drag his chief across the uneven ground. A few moments before, he had woken in a cramped corner of the cave, his head spinning with dreams. He was cold and weak with hunger. Looking at the ring of fires, he wished he was closer to their warmth.

He looked up into the sky. The ice-eye was closed tonight but the small ones were open, glittering like insects. Esk pressed himself to the cold stone. Richard stayed back as far as he could, not wanting to be part of the savagery that was in the air. To Richard it seemed that Esk could escape and he was at a loss to understand why the caveboy did not sneak away into the forests.

The stone pressed back in a Mother's embrace. So long as Esk kept well clear of the open the Lundren could not harm him. (Richard understood now and was faintly disgusted with his soul-mate's cowardice.) The Lundren had killed many of Esk's tribe and there was no wish on his part to join them. He wanted to be born again as a tree or a bush – something hanging in the wind, like hair across the Mother's face, brushing Her brow. As a tree he would not have to hunt or fight. He could stand tall and survey the world, his spirit locked inside a strong body. If the stone Lundren took him now he would become part of them. Part of the dark, sinister ring of night creatures formed out of cold rock. They had no souls, nor warmth in their eyes. The Lundren spoke in harsh tones – they did not whisper in the Mother's sweet breath as did the leaves of the trees.

(Richard realized as the images came to him that he was wrong to call Esk a coward. Esk was merely one of his kind: a superstitious primitive man. But he was also one of the first men. His body juices ran thick and rich. He was the bloodstock of the human race, which thrived on savage sports, hand to hand combat, hunting and racing flat-out across the courtyard of the early world. Esk lived in a time long before old and fair-skinned men with automatic weapons slayed the fittest cat, a big-bossed buffalo and deer. Esk was the essence of the fat aristocrats of the twentieth century; those creatures who, sweating gin and tonic, smoky-lunged and bored with all but death, went tramping through the bush to stem the strongest breath. Those later men created a new law of the jungle – the survival of Man.)

Since the new experience of travel to another place had entered his life, Esk, quite naturally, had rationalized the seeming reality of the dream-world by forming comparisons with his own world and allowing for subtle differences. Richard was unafraid of the night, yet frequently withdrew during the daylight hours. (Esk had felt the Other's strange revulsion of the hunt and his unnatural abhorrence of violence.) It was therefore fairly obvious that there was a reversal of roles of the occupants in Richard's world. The daytime was when the loathsome stone creatures crawled out of their holes and swallowed men whole and rocks distorted themselves, growing large malevolent heads with shining eyes. Richard's body was a fortunate host because Richard was himself a magician, well able to cope with these distortions of the Mother. In fact, the dark thought had crossed Esk's mind once or twice, probably Richard was himself one of those blackrock sorcerers. He did, after all, hide in a cave – a cave with no opening – during the night.

Esk was no coward. Just a mortal youth living in a time when sorcery and evil were unharnessed by scientific reason.

They dragged the dead Shaman's body into the cave as Skell was weeping for his friend and lieutenant, the brave but foolish Crak. The mighty frame of Crak lay beside one of the fires, its eyes staring out into the speckled blackness of the night, seeing nothing. Now Skell would eat the brains of his second-in-command, as a tribute to the man who had been such a loyal and faithful follower of his Shaman.

"I will see you avenged, my friend," vowed Skell, well within earshot of his young men. "And you will walk beside me still, in spirit. The night cannot hold your spirit down. I shall paint a picture of your greatest deeds. . . ." Suddenly the god's divine eye appeared and shone its light directly into Skell's own eyes. He felt himself falling, sprawling over the prostrate body of the dead Crak. The light burned into his brain and he fought to push it out. At the last moment before blackness descended a voice screamed at him and he knew that Crak had reached out of the kingdom of the dead and was berating Skell in his high death voice for making him fight the Shaman of the resident group. Crak was having his revenge.

When sensibility found a place in his mind once more Skell staggered to his feet. It was early morning and the fires had died out around him. One or two of his young bodyguards were still with him but most had disappeared – probably they were asleep. Skell felt sick and his head was buzzing with the sound of the insects that sang around bad meat.

"Fetch me some water," he croaked, sitting down abruptly on the chest of his old friend.

The flesh was cold on his buttocks and Skell rose again, delicately, to sit down upon the warm ashes of the nearest fireplace. He considered vaguely that he would need to eat Crak's brains fairly soon or the insects really would be humming their death song in the ear of the corpse. Probably for breakfast except that he did not feel at all like eating food of any kind.

Water duly arrived and Skell settled the queaziness with several noisy gulps. He stared moodily at his former friend's shell. Frost had crept into the blanket of bristle on the chin and filled the nostril hair with tiny glittering stones. The tusk had been removed from the chest of the corpse and the blood had dried into a crusty river which formed its delta somewhere inside the matted fur of the loin cloth. The hands were curled, like dead white spiders with stocky legs and those famous knees that had felled many an opponent were bent almost double: the final convulsion. He looks like a baby, thought

Skell. Not a dead man. Now Crak had jumped inside Skell's head and the two of them would share the same body. That was all right because it meant that Skell would inherit Crak's fighting skills.

A small bird landed on the face of the corpse, its feet planted firmly on the left cheekbone. It began to sing its high-pitched mountain song. Skell reached forward to snatch at the creature – not because its act was disrespectful: his instincts were testing an old skill. Once, when a young man, he could have caught it in flight – provided it was within reach. He would have plucked it out of the air as it flew past his ear. This time he missed. A sitting target too! He was getting old.

The smell of ozone was heavy in the air. There must have been a storm during the night. It might have been wise to send some of the woman down to the seashore to pick up any shellfish that may have been washed ashore. There would be seaweed too, which was pleasant when roasted over a fire.

He bored his buttocks deeper into the ashes as he was reminded that the outer layer had cooled. The warmth it gave him was only local, admittedly, and more than once he had singed the hair around the lower regions of his abdomen, but it was a pleasure for which he was willing to make sacrifices. He *was* getting old.

The sounds of activity began to penetrate the morning air: the clink of stone on stone, the sound of stone on wood, horn on bone; the human sounds of nose and throat clearings, passing wind and the inevitable chatter and double-chatter over the heads of crying children. Like most intelligent introspective politicians, Skell, having passed the second phase of his Stone Age life, was wondering whether it was all worth it. Being a leader was going to be twice as hard without Crak and the whole business of giving orders was beginning to become a thorough nuisance. The excitement from the feeling of power it once gave him, had palled long before Crak's death. He thought he might give up and live a solitary existence somewhere in the mountains above. Take a woman, perhaps, but having only responsibility for one's own family. Trouble was, he could not stand to see anyone else giving the orders. It made his blood hot and his whole disposition uncomfortably violent.

Now he had Crak trying to push his way in. Well, that was another aspect altogether. No one was going to take over the body of Skell without a battle. Not even Crak.

Skell then ate some breakfast and, with Crak's dead eyes still staring at the clouds through crooked legs, he entered the cave to paint the demise of his lieutenant.

Skell had already painted the pre-event picture. It remained to add the heroes of the hour as in any pictorial representation. The pre-battle or pre-hunt mural was a magic rite to sway the skull-god in favour of the righteous. Afterwards, to keep the record straight, specific occurrences were superimposed upon the ordained scene.

Esk and Richard shared the eyes: Richard because he was fascinated by the scene of a cave artist at work, and Esk because he was watching for a chance to escape, although he too realized he was privileged in witnessing the Shaman at work.

The body of the caveboy was lying in a dark corner of the cavern, away from the tallow lamp fashioned from a hollow stone. The atmosphere in the cavern was thick and had a drugging effect on the brain shared by the two youths. They watched as the old woman, who had pushed hard red berries into her eye sockets, presumably to give herself the look of a succubus, mixed animal fat with powders already occupying snail shells. Since she was blind Richard assumed that it must have been one of the other Neanderthals that originally ground the powders. From his father's lunch-table chats he knew the powders to be ochres, manganese and possibly pipeclay or slaked lime. (He had taken an interest in these talks since art was one of the subjects at which he excelled.)

The ochres would produce several colours from yellow to sepia, purplish-red and brown; the manganese, black and blueblack. Richard wondered what sort of instrument would be used to apply the paints.

Eventually the artist entered. Esk recognized him as the

Shaman of the tribe and his heart began to beat a little faster. He was afraid of the evil-looking little man. An Agril must have spawned such a squat ugly body. The Shaman appeared to be very nervous, glancing over his shoulder occasionally and running his eyes over the high ceiling of the cavern where the shadows, caused by the lamp, danced and swayed.

The old woman was muttering to herself as she rattled a stick inside the giant shells. The Shaman growled something at her and she eventually fell silent, though with obvious reluctance.

The paintbrush was revealed to be a twig, chewed at one end to produce a fibrous tip. On the wall the artist had already sketched a scene in charcoal but the figures were scratchy stick-like affairs with little pretence at following human anatomy. Not like Granla's paintings, thought Esk, which had beautiful rounded contours.

Even so Esk marvelled at the strokes of the Shaman of the ugly people. The paints were applied liberally as he smeared the surface of the cave wall with thick red daubs. A lot of red was used and black. The colours of blood and death. Not a happy painting. The man that died must have been a close friend of the Shaman. Yellow was hardly in evidence. Little brightness came from the picture.

Richard came forward, smelling in Esk's nostrils the pungent tallow fat burning the air inside the cave, absorbing every detail of the scene before him. It was a dark, mystical experience – not unlike his visit to the Chinese Buddhist temple as a boy of six years. (The scene of that visit drifted through his mind and he could smell again the atmosphere of the cells within the building; could picture the heavy red drapes patterned with yellow Chinese characters, each one of which was in itself several clashing golden sword blades.) Everything in the cave oozed the dark secrets of the dead, gave out the heavy smell of an alien magic. The low flame of the lamp closeted the two figures in a prison of light, walls of darkness moving in and out, pulsating, alive. It was 33,000 years ago, down the tunnel of time.

Suddenly the crone stood up and shuffled out, leaving the Shaman alone. The man stepped backwards, admiring his work. It looked crude alongside the Cro-Magnon paintings but it had its own charisma. A more primitive style but still it captured the essence of the theme — the life and death throes of two heroes: Granla and the Neanderthal. It depicted nothing of the truth. The two burnt-stick figures were leaping high in the air, each with a spear about to impale the other. They looked like two thin shadows intoxicated with the fever of a dance: heads back, limbs in action poses, spears descending. Richard was reminded of the Watutsi lion hunting tribal dance pictures from his geography tapes. Only the iron-red wash of blood in the background brought home the awfulness of the dancers' real intentions.

Esk was reluctant to admit that the painting of the dwarf had anything to commend it. He nursed a distinct loathing for the little man and everything he represented.

The artist turned, and suddenly he looked directly at the spot where the caveboy's body lay. He stared, and as he did so a shuddering flowed through his frame. His movements quickened and the head swivelled, looking around the cavern. Suddenly they fixed themselves on an object some inches away from the Shaman's nose. He jumped backwards. It was a large cave spider, balanced upon the tip of a stalagmite. The paintbrush stick whipped out and the creature was transfixed, wriggling, on the point of the limestone cone. The Shaman then moved away, towards the cave entrance. After a few moments he had disappeared from the sight of the youths' one pair of eyes.

Not good, thought Esk. These dwarves are bad people.

Why?

They kill harmless cave spiders. Spiders that help to keep the living places free from the annoying flies.

Perhaps he is unused to caves?

Then he is a savage, replied Esk.

Yes, answered Richard gravely, mental tongue in cheek. *A barbarian.*

155

An idea came to Richard. He desperately wanted to prove to his father that he had been back to the Pleistocene era. Coming forward he took over from Esk and then dipped his finger in some of the red ochre. Under the drawing of the two stick men he wrote RICHARD in recognizable letters. Let them find that in the future, he thought, and they will not be able to dispute that I was ever here.

Esk came forward to look. Criss-cross markings? Magic symbols? He shrugged. Richard slipped back again, satisfied with his one contribution to the world of cave art.

Esk's next consideration was to get back to his own group. Clearly it was not going to be possible to do so in the light of the fire-eye. He was going to have to escape just before dawn, so that the Lundren were at least on their flight back to their perches inside the rock.

It was obvious that the dwarves would be attacking the Gren before long. He had to get back to warn them as soon as possible. Hungry as he was, if he showed himself to the dwarves and reminded them of his presence they would be sure to initiate some distasteful entertainment for themselves with Esk as the main event. He could get water from the teeth of rock hanging from the ceiling of the cavern but food was another matter.

Then he remembered the tallow candle burning in the stone lamp. He crossed the floor and extinguished the wick, taking it out of the pot. Then he drank the warm fat, feeling it slide down into his belly. It was good. Afterwards he licked at the pools of water that filled small hollows in the floor. There were also some bones which the dwarves had left lying around. There was no meat on them but he gathered up one or two, feeling his way around in the darkness. Then he found his way to the rear exit and squeezed through into the secondary cavern, taking care to keep to the walls once inside. When the dwarves had gone, or had been killed, Esk would return for the body of Granla and bury it, near the rock shelter, in the bosom of the Mother.

Esk even contemplated killing the Shaman of the dwarves while that ugly hogface slept. Then to drag him into the secondary cavern and drop him down the hole into the Mother's bowels. That would be a fitting resting place for the hated one, amongst the Mother's faeces — especially since he seemed to dislike caves so much. To drop him into a hole to stay for all eternity. That was a joke the whole of Gren would enjoy.

He was on the point of attempting to carry out his plan, when Richard had to intervene.

No, it would be stupid.

Why? questioned Esk.

Because I know. Don't question me. I'm thousands of years older than you are.

You are the magician of dreams?

Yes. If you go out there I will leave you to your fate. You'll be hung from a tree by your heels and smeared with honey. The hornets will sting you to death. It was the worst thing Richard could think of but it meant nothing to Esk. However, he stayed anyway. His mood of revenge had dissipated during the argument. The important thing was to reach the group once again. He slept, with Richard remaining awake and staring into the darkness, tired of adventures and longing for a normal life once again.

Esk jerked awake in the darkness of a tomb. Then he remembered and knew it was almost dawn outside the caverns. He knew because he knew. It was that instinct lost by Richard and the Modern men. He knew as a flower knows, and begins to open; as a laboratory-held mollusc, far from its sea bed, knows that the tide should have covered its lair of silt; as the wintering badger in its home below the earth knows that spring is near: by the natural rhythmic clock of his body, by a subtle change in temperature not registered by any instrument of man, by the magnetic patterns of the Mother and Her Paleolithic ice-eye. It *was* near the dawn.

Esk cracked open the bones he had taken the previous night and sucked the marrow from them. He thought again about those strange marks his hands had written on the wall. He was beginning to become a fully-fledged Shaman without even wanting to do so. Perhaps a man may never escape his fate? If the Mother wished him to be a Shaman, he would become one — whether he wished it for himself or not.

He found his way to the cavern's rear entrance and crawled along until he could smell the clean air. It was still quite dark but there was the light of the fire-eye in a corner of the sky. He would wait just a little longer before sneaking through the sentries and slipping into the thick forests.

He waited.

A little while later he judged it safe to leave the protection of the Mother. The Lundren would be *en route* for their perches. They would have no time to stop and sink their massive stone claws into a running caveboy. Esk began to creep out, between the sleeping bodies that lay around the clearing. There were one or two sentries standing on the pale of the area, as Esk had guessed there would be, but it was near the end of their watch — they would be heavy-eyed and careless. Esk never attempted more than a few yards at a time, pausing to lay among the bodies as if asleep. Fortunately, if any sentries had glanced his way they would notice no difference between Esk and their own people for the youth was of a similar height.

Once, he slipped down softly beside a woman. She subsequently stirred her ankle crossing his and remaining there. Irrepressible panic rose in his chest which sent a scarlet haze through Richard's thoughts. If he was caught lying locked to one of the tribe's females he would be beaten to death. Her man would make sure of that. He looked at the girl. Her mouth hung open and her wide rows of teeth misted over as she exhaled the cold morning air. The ankle locked with his was booted in fur but she still might feel him move.

Blow into her nostrils, Richard advised, having tried the trick once on a pet dog that whimpered in its sleep.

Esk did as he was told and the girl grunted, grumbled in the back of her throat, and rolled away. Esk was on his feet in a split second and into the thickly wooded area. He whispered softly to them, once hidden, asking the tree spirits to be his friends and to keep him safe from the unbelievers, the heathens. One or two whispered in reply and Esk afforded himself a smile. They were men like him, after all, beneath those wooden exteriors.

Inside the cloak of the forest Esk felt more at ease. Richard, too, had always had an affinity with trees. As a child he had played in a partly shaded garden and the feeling of lying below the gentle shoulders of an oak was as soothing as it was secure. He had no names for the trees under which Esk led him, but they seemed little different from those of a Cyprus in the future. They were more closely knit than any trees he had known before, and there was a blackness as thick as estuary mud below their branches. Esk found his way only by the feel of a much-used path beneath his feet.

Esk was in a great hurry. He felt sure that once the dwarves (who were not really as small as the Agril but it suited him to insult them as such) found he was missing they would know the Gren was alerted and would be down on them like Lundren under the ice-eye. The caveboy wondered who was acting in the place of the Shaman now that Granla was missing. Reng, probably. He was not the largest nor strongest of the Gren but he was most definitely a savage and terrible fighter.

Lelka would be anxious for news of Esk too. He had a certain affection for his wizened old mother and it upset him to think she would be worried. Many youths discarded any fondness for their mothers once they reached their middle age. Esk was at pains not to display too much outward affection but he knew that he was too soft inside to be a Shaman. It was probably a good thing for the tribe that it was not to be. Granla had left him too early, too soon.

Suddenly he came upon one of those clearings which, in Cyprus, are caused by the underlying rock being closed to the surface and leaving no depth of soil to which a tree can cling. There were one or two tough old conifers, that balanced themselves, flatfooted, on top of the balding area but these had sent out roots like snakes in search of cracks and holes, into many of which they dipped their tips. Where the rock itself rippled through the white and green it occasionally carried with it a single nest of flowers: ears protruding from the Mother's bare skull.

The sky was now alight with the flames of the fire-eye and Esk felt it was safe enough to cross the space in the forest. He was an extremely cautious youth where the supernatural was concerned and he meant to take absolutely no risks. He ran like a deer.

The crossing safely over he threw himself into the forest again, forded a freezing stream and came out into an even larger clearing. Home was not too far distant. He only had to cross the mountains.

Richard was asleep: lulled into a dreamless state by the complacent Esk.

Esk had begun to move out into the clearing when his acute senses warned him that something or someone was nearby. Immediately a chill of fear woke Richard and Esk stood stonestill, waiting for recognition of the plight in which he stood. Was it the Short Ones? The thought went to Richard, who imagined the five-feet tall Shaman of the Neanderthals blocking their way to freedom and safety: the vicious smile came readily to mind, the thick brutal arms, the heavy legs with their scarred horny feet. Richard remembered, too, those fists of the previous evening, as the stone axes bludgeoned the Cro-Magnon Shaman to death: hammers within hammers. And the eyes. Above all Richard remembered the eyes.

Into the trees!

Wait! returned Esk, calmer than the other youth within his frame, we might be turning into danger.

Esk's body waited.

After a long while the leaves of the trees to the left of Esk parted and a young man stepped out. His body was decked with colourful war paint and he carried his spear with the tip of chalcedony in his right hand. In his left was a heavy club.

"Reng," cried Esk in a relieved tone, "I've found you."

The two youths stepped towards each other. Reng's face was hidden beneath the dyes of his magic battle face.

"And I have found you," he said.

Then with two swings of the club he brought Esk to his knees.

"Reng," mumbled Esk, the blood from his wounds filling his eyes, "I must tell you . . ." The club came down a third time and the light of the Mother's fire-eye fled from the brain of Esk. His half-brother, Ring-around-the-ice-eye, had had his revenge.

11

Reng and the warriors of the Gren met a party of the Newcomers that had been sent out to find Esk and take him back to Skell. Thinking they had surprised the main war party of the enemy, Reng's men fell on this group and a fierce battle began. The two species of Paleolithic Man met in a splintering of stone on stone, and while the Northerners were not as well armed as their opponents the numbers were fairly even and the newcomers from the continent were a stronger, hardier breed than the islander types. What they lacked in stature they made up for in viciousness and muscle.

Reng's sagacity turned him into a legend. As Shaman he took the initiative by leaping up and standing on the shoulders of the nearest opponent, and with the man's head held between Reng's ankles he drove the spear downwards directly into the top of the skull.

The Northerners had obviously fought many people during their march southwards and before long Reng and his men found themselves hardpressed, despite the fact that the enemy had been surprised and were without the protection of magic symbols on their bodies. Finally the Gren resorted to an old trick of theirs of running into the forest and climbing the trees. When the triumphant Newcomers followed, the Gren dropped onto their shoulders and locked their legs around the Northerners' necks. Individual battles ensued and finally the remainder of the Newcomers retreated to report to their Shaman. One man remained a captive of the Gren.

Reng and his Gren, believing that they had administered a sound thrashing to their enemy, gathered together their wounded, picked up their two dead warriors, and made their own way back to the rock shelter. Reng said nothing to the other men about his encounter with Esk: they were not permitted to ask. Esk had passed by them as they lay on either side of the path between the two clearings and Reng had followed him alone. Esk's body had been dragged back into the trees. Later Reng would return and give his brother a decent burial. It had not been a religious crime for the youth to rival Reng for leadership – he was therefore entitled to be placed inside the Mother.

The fire-eye threw golden light upon the warpainted faces of the Gren as they marched back into the rock shelter. With them was their captive. Later they would return for the corpses of the dead Northerners, to save the bodies from the beasts if they could. They were all children of the Mother, even though the dwarves were as ugly as the Agril.

12

"The bastard's got my baby — they've taken my girl!" McKinnon was shouting out of the visiphone screen at Levan.

Levan had just been for a long walk on the beach. He still had not contacted anyone in the medical profession outside Cyprus. The boy's condition was no better than in the beginning. Now McKinnon was having apoplexy over something that appeared to be nothing to do with Levan.

"Stop yelling, McKinnon — just calm down," said Levan. "What the hell is this all about? What girl?" He had vague thoughts of the Canadian authorities jailing or impounding one of McKinnon's erstwhile mistresses.

The impetus of McKinnon's first rush of words carried him rapidly into the follow-up.

"The Xen's grabbed my daughter. I'm in trouble, Levan. I need money fast. These people are vicious — even if they don't kill her, they might . . . they might hurt her badly. They're animals, some of them. . . ."

Something clicked in Levan's head and the realization locked his vocal cords for a second.

"Rosemary's been kidnapped? Where's Loraine?" he finally said.

"She's here, pretty busted up. . . ."

"What!" Levan was shouting now. "What do you mean, 'busted up'?"

Levan's anger seemed to have a calming effect on McKinnon, as if some of the responsibility which had been heavy on his conscience, had undergone a transfer.

"Emotionally — I'm talking about emotionally. She hasn't been touched physically, thank God. I'd've killed him if he'd . . ."

"But he's taken Rosemary. Where?"

"If I knew that I wouldn't be calling you. I thought . . ." he waved his hands wildly. "I thought he might try to kill *me* — I didn't realize my girls were in danger. How could I? I'd no idea. I tell you I thought he would try and take *me* and I was ready for him," McKinnon finished defensively.

"They're not *your* girls," replied Levan coldly. "Not any more. However, I can understand how you feel. I don't see how I can help but I'll do my best. Have you called the police?"

"Loraine did that. They've been and gone and they weren't very helpful."

"They'll do what they can. You're lucky — it's a small island and he's a stranger, isn't he? You said he was Spanish-speaking?"

A Xen could have been anything from a Puerto Rican to a Mexican so far as McKinnon was concerned.

"Yes, I think so. I'm sure of it."

Levan continued, "Well, there aren't many places he can hide for long — unless he's prepared some place with food and water beforehand. I'll get my man, Kariyos. He'll contact some of his people and scour this part of the island. The police will be looking too. Let's hope he won't harm her. I suppose he's expecting you to get some money together?"

"I suppose so," McKinnon answered dully.

"Well, I'll do that. What did you drop?"

McKinnon told him and he whistled.

"No wonder they're after your guts. They'll want more than that now. They've been put to a certain amount of expense and trouble. Probably triple the original debt. I don't know if I can raise it. . . ."

"He's already called us. The original debt has had a hundred and fifty percent interest added. You must be worth that much."

"It's not in hard cash you ignorant sod," snapped Levan.

"Sell something then."

"Let me speak to Loraine," replied Levan firmly.

Loraine's face appeared. Bitter lines curved into the corners of the mouth.

"What happened, Lorrie?" he asked gently.

"Someone met her from school," replied Loraine in a dull voice. "As she came out of the building someone ... Alan knows the man. She was pulled into a parked slider and driven away. Before her friends could fetch help he must have been well on his way into the mountains."

"Mountains? – why do you say that?"

"Because he called me later and Rosemary, behind him, shouted something about a mountain. He won't be there now, of course. He doesn't even need to collect the money. What he asked for was for the debt to be repaid. That is, Alan has to ensure that a certain bank account is credited with the right figures."

She turned her head away from the screen.

"What was that?" asked Levan, aware that something had distracted her.

"Alan left." She stared downwards for a moment, then added, "Nothing important."

"Give me the account number and I'll put into it what I have. It's a pity I've just paid the Cyprus authorities for the power I used for the repeater. Still, I'll do what I can. At least they'll see that we're serious. In the meantime Kariyos will, I'm sure, get his family and friends organized into a search party. Don't worry – we'll find her."

Loraine looked tired and beaten.

"Thank you, Paul. I shan't forget this."

"I won't let you," he replied. "Get over here." He switched off the set.

Kariyos was located at his favourite bar and listened thoughtfully to what was said. The background noise was irritating to Levan but he did his best to hide it.

"We find this man," Kariyos replied at length. "We find him but we do nothing. This is best. I will ask many people. Some of those who work in the fields will have seen some-

166

things. Then I tell you and you must do what you will. Okay?"

The grizzled face was full of confidence. Levan hoped it was not alcoholically induced.

"Okay. Thanks. Call this number. I'd like to be out there helping but it's best someone stays here in a central position today. Tomorrow I'll help."

"Okay, yes. Like headquarters. I call you." The face disappeared.

Levan heaved a sigh of relief. At least this was giving him something on which to concentrate. God, that was bad. That was not the way to consider the situation at all. True, though. The skeletons had been crated and were on their way to a buyer and all that was left was for Levan to think about Richard's condition. Levan's thought patterns over the last week or two had adopted an iterative motion of their own – like waves falling one after another onto the flat sands of his mind. His brain was numbed into lethargy.

He considered what McKinnon's next move would be. Probably he would disappear into the Oriental Maze – that conglomerate group of East Asian states with ill-defined borders, into which a person who wished to disappear might slip and never be seen again. Therein lay the drawback. The fragmented little countries were always at war with their neighbours and anyone entering the fiasco of guerilla and counter-guerilla warfare, some of whose combatants hardly knew which side they were on from one day to the next, ran the risk of involvement. In fact it was impossible to prevent being forced to take sides, and strangers tended to be used as scapegoats. McKinnon, Levan reflected, might just as well hand himself over to his persecutors. The little warring factions of the East had long since ceased to be policed by the United World Forces and had been given up for lost – sealed from without and left to fester in isolation, like a contained sore on an otherwise relatively healthy body. The seal could be penetrated, though, if someone was determined enough: just as, in the old days, a man could slip away into the backstreets of a shanty-town. It was the many rivers that afforded entrance from the sea to the Oriental Maze, by junk or sampan.

The door to the bungalow slid open and interrupted his thoughts. Loraine entered the room. Her face looked calm but he noticed her hands were shaking violently.

"Sit down, Loraine," he said, "I'll get you a drink." Overwrought women embarrassed him.

"Thanks," she replied. "I'll be all right, Paul. Please don't fuss too much. I *will* be okay."

"No doubt," he said. "But I need a drink too. Richard's still as bad as he was," he added, hoping to take her mind away from her own troubles.

She nodded. "Perhaps," she said in a faraway voice, "we're both destined to lose our children."

Levan's head snapped backwards. "What do you mean 'lose'?"

"Perhaps they'll both die. Not many kidnapped children survive, you know – the statistics . . ."

"This is different," he said quickly. "The man has no need to kill Rosemary. Alan knows what he looks like – so do you. You saw him on the visiphone. They only kill their victims when they're afraid of being recognized by them later. . . ."

"Maybe. I . . . I don't know."

"And Richard?" he foolishly asked. "What about him?"

"Well, the caveboy died young. You found the bones."

Feeling uneasy he pressed her further although he knew he would not like the answer. He himself had been pricked by fears of a similar nature. Previously he had cast them aside before they took root.

"And what then?"

"Richard says he is in the brain of the Paleolithic boy. I believe he is. What happens when that boy dies – in his own time? Perhaps both hearts will stop beating at once."

"Rubbish," he snapped.

Loraine said quietly. "Well, I hope so. I do hope so, Paul. We both love our children, after all."

The following morning Levan was out in the foothills with Kariyos and his men. It was early and there was some dew on the crisp remnants of the winter foliage. He was glad to concentrate on something other than his son's predicament. He had put on his climbing boots and the wetness transferred itself to them from the thistles and shone from their caps. He felt they looked a bit incongruous with the khaki shorts and shirt but he carried no weapons – did not expect to be in the position where he would have to use one – and the boots were comfortably heavy. No, comforting was the word. If, just if, he did get himself into a situation from which he found it necessary to escape the boots might help him, in some way.

All through the hills there were men searching. A shepherd had seen the pair struggling up a slope in this area – the man pulling the girl. He had thought they were lovers.

"Jesus Christ," Levan had said, throwing his hands up in a gesture illustrating his exasperation, "doesn't he know the difference between a fourteen-year-old girl and a grown woman?"

"These people?" Kariyos had exclaimed, then, seeing Levan's puzzled expression, added a flat, "No."

Kariyos was now to his left, about 500 yards away. He could see the old man moving with solid limbs along a goat track. Here and there were police from both sides of the fence, but no soldiers. It was a large island and not everyone took notice of a shepherd. Some of the authorities were convinced that the kidnapper had had a skipboat hidden on the headland and was now somewhere off the coast of Turkey. That was where they were concentrating their efforts.

"Shouldn't we be in a line?" shouted Levan to the nearest bunch of men. The whole method of search seemed wrong to him. It consisted of knots of people moving aimlessly, or so it seemed, back and forth over the same ground.

The men swung round and looked towards the shouter but after they had turned back he received no more attention. Barflies, he thought to himself. Boozy old guys with no other aim in life than to fill the toothless hole amongst their white-

169

needled faces with wine — or, if they were Turkish Cypriots, coffee. Those men had worn the same old shapeless clothes since the beginning of time. Their skins, creased and weathered, had been the colour of mahogany before the making of the sun. Their short bristled heads had lolled, heavy with rustic knowledge, over the Creator, watching with patronizing interest as he pieced together the universe.

"Those old bastards shouldn't even be out here," shouted Levan to Kariyos ungraciously.

Kariyos waved and Levan realized he should not be making the noise he was. If the kidnapper was near he might be armed. Probably was. Levan was making a fool of himself and Kariyos would probably tell him so later.

He kicked over a stone and a small black snake wriggled blindly out into the sun. Levan jumped back because he was not sure whose side the snake was on, but he was used to them. They invaded his diggings often enough. He looked above him. Sure enough a predator was wheeling in the air. The snake would need to find another rock soon or become buzzard bait.

The search continued throughout the day without success and when the evening came Levan had to report the failure to Loraine. He had half-hoped to see Rosemary sitting beside her mother, having been released or found by another party. It was a faint hope, he knew, and it was not realized. When he entered the bungalow Loraine was sitting quietly in a chair, her hands clasped in her lap like a nun meditating. She did not even turn her head as he walked to her.

"You didn't find her," she said. A statement, not a question. Levan's throat was suddenly very dry.

"There's tomorrow. We covered a lot of ground today. We'll find her. I'll go out early." His head was pounding from a day under the sun, even though he had worn a hat.

"Yes, I will," he said. "But I think I'll lie down now. My head hurts. Call me at six. I won't eat anything. I'll have a large breakfast. We'll find her, don't worry. And the money's in a bank account — a little of it. I have my agents working on the rest."

Her tone reflected her despair. "But does he know that?"

At that point the visiphone buzzed. Loraine switched it on quickly, her face flushed. The look faded when she saw it was the doctor at Akrotiri hospital.

"Mrs McKinnon? I was told you might know where Mr Levan is."

Levan stepped in front of the bright purple camera light perched on top of the instrument.

"I'm here," he said, before she could answer.

The face on the screen was expressionless.

"Can you get over here as soon as you can, Mr Levan? There's been ..." he coughed, "... there's been an unusual, well, yes, a very unusual development. One I wasn't expecting at all. ..."

13

Esk regained consciousness gradually, swinging in and out of awareness almost in time with the rhythms of his pain. The final blow which Reng had administered to the side of his face had broken his jaw; he could feel the looseness of the piece of bone that swam freely in his flesh. There was also an area of hurt in his hand: probably a broken finger. He must have fallen awkwardly.

Raising himself on his elbow he attempted to focus on his surroundings but there was a distortion – some of the shapes were ill-defined. He could see the trees – solid shapes around him – but there were other objects, insubstantial phantoms of artifacts Esk had seen in Richard's time. He could also see parts of Richard's body mingling with his own, just as the spirits of objects from Richard's cave hung like mist in the branches of the trees. There was the ghost of a man, staring at him, hard, its hands clasped together.

The ghost that had captured Esk's pain-filled eyes was Paul Levan, superimposed with the rest of the scene within Richard's vision, upon the Pleistocene day.

Richard himself was alert and subject, distantly, to the pain of his friend. He was lying on his hospital bed with his father sitting beside him, but the intangible shapes of Paleolithic Man's forest growth came up through the floor and disappeared into the white-washed ceiling – the tree-top waved some way above the roof of the building. There were the translucent ghosts of birds flying between the branches of the trees and small creatures in the leaves.

Richard reached back into Esk for a moment and gasped at

the force of Esk's pain, though he could hear his father calling for a doctor; watched him press a bell above the bed.

"Don't let them put me to sleep," he begged. "Please, Dad, please. If you do I'll die with Esk. Don't let them, please don't let them."

His father gripped his hand, the eyes full of anxiety and pity.

"We might have to, Richard. You'll be fine – you'll see."

"Dad – please!" he shouted at his father. "I need Esk. I need him." He panted, withdrawing from the pain. "You don't know what it's like. Listen, it's Esk that's hurt, not me – but I can't get away from the pain completely. I'm asking you, don't let them do anything to me."

A nurse entered the room and Richard contrived to appear relaxed and well. He smiled at her, controlling the turbulence within him.

"It's all right. Those ghosts I was telling the doctor about earlier. They've gone now. I just want to talk to my father."

The nurse, enveloped within a phantom trunk, smiled back.

"You were very frightened."

"Well, I'm not any more. I feel better now my father's here."

The effort at maintaining a polite attitude towards the nurse was becoming too much for him.

She looked at Levan, who nodded briefly. A moment later she had gone.

Richard lay back on his pillow with a sigh of relief.

After a few moments Levan asked, "What do you want to do?"

"Just wait," replied Richard. "Wait until something happens. It won't end here."

"I know that," said his father, "but I'm very worried. I – I just don't *know*."

It was a crisp, dry morning with a light breeze blowing. Esk staggered to his feet and vomited the thin slimy contents of his stomach onto the ferns. For a while the retching continued, wrenching at his stomach muscles, until nothing came up any more. He gripped a tree, hugging it to him, then began to move off in the direction taken by Reng – back towards the Cave of Paintings and the dwarf-men. He was not sure what he wanted to do, but if Reng was painted for war he must have had other warriors nearby. If he could find them, and explain, they might carry him home. Otherwise he would die. His head hurt badly and the shapes of Richard's cave artifacts did nothing but hinder his orientation. The ghost still stared, its drawn and ghoulish face hovering over him.

He propelled himself from tree to tree, occasionally pausing to let another heaving fit pass or to regain sensibility from a bout of dizziness. If he met a savage beast now he knew he would be finished. Richard appeared to be watching his progress and giving encouragement, though he seemed distant. Perhaps he was trying to retreat from the pain?

Reng was now Shaman, he guessed, and would have to be placated. Then again he might be dead. All the warriors might be dead! The thought filled the caveboy with horror.

Finally he came near to the clearing just before the cave and fell down, dragging himself slowly through the vegetation to the edge of the trees. The dry coldness in the ground bit into his skin and stiff grasses pierced the bare part of his body.

"Stim! He's near the cave," said Richard excitedly. "He's going back to the cave. He'll be killed!"

"Let's just wait, son, like you said. Watch and wait."

"Yes, that's it," nodded Richard. "That's it, Dad."

Esk parted the bushes. The scene that met his and Richard's eyes filled both youths with consternation. The whole tribe of the Neanderthals was decked for war and they were gathered in a ring around their Shaman, chanting in low voices as he raised and lowered their totem skull. Reng and the others must have met resistance, thought Esk, and returned to the rock shelter. Then the youth saw several bodies laid out by the fire and realized a battle had already taken place. The dwarf-men were going out to seek revenge.

The pain was sweeping through him in waves now as he

stared towards the Cave of Paintings. He was dying and there was no one who could help him any more. The only real regret he had was that he had never killed a savage beast, or a man in battle, in single combat. He had killed fierce animals as part of a team, using devices such as staked pits – but never with a weapon, alone and unaided. It was a bitter feeling, having to return to the Mother without ever proving his worth. He was going as a child, not a man.

Richard struggled upright and said to Levan, "We've got to get to the cave, Dad. I think I can find it now, with Esk's eyes. If we can get there we may be able to help him."

"Richard – are you sure . . . well, how *can* you help him? You live thousands of years apart. It's . . . *it's got to be your imagination. Believe me!*"

Richard said, "Dad. You want me to get better? *I* want to get better. This is the closest I've been to parting from Esk since the accident. I feel we're on the verge of separating – yet I don't want to leave him to die, friendless. I'm confusing him by being so far from him – geographically. We came together – our minds fused – when we stood on the same patch of earth, past and future. Perhaps if we can get together at the same place now we can part company. That's two good reasons for going, Dad – don't make me ask you any more – his hurt is bad enough as it is."

His father watched him for a few moments as distant pains struck, ravaged, and then subsided. Levan appeared to make a decision.

"Get your shorts on, son," he said. "We'll have to sneak out the back way. But God help me – and you – if we're wrong to be taking you away like this."

Richard punched lightly at the scar his teeth had left on his father's chin. It was a gesture he had not used in a long time.

"We're not wrong, Dad. It's nearly over – I know it." One way or the other, he thought.

"Okay, let's go."

Physically weak, Richard had to be helped down to the

slider. As he lowered himself through the hatchway his father said, "We'll stop by a bar and collect Kariyos. I don't want us to get lost in the mountains. Where is this cave — approximately?"

"From here — uh, north-east. In the foothills of the Troodos range — before the coast."

"That's a big area."

"We'll find it."

"You hope."

Esk began to feel himself growing stronger as Richard drew closer to the place where he lay. The contours of the land heaved like the sea mother in a ghost-like dance and his friend's companions rode her waves inside their floating monster. The dwarves had left the village, their women-folk having gone with them, prepared to camp — to follow into the very heart of the battle. Esk felt he had to do something — anything — to warn his people. The only person left in the clearing was the blind old crone he had seen in the cave, helping the Shaman with his painting. She had alone remained behind to tend the fires. At that moment she was gathering up sticks from the woodpile and feeling her way back to the warmth of the flames.

Esk staggered out into the clearing.

What are you doing? Richard questioned Esk. He could see the fires raging in the caveboy's mind, reaching to the sky. They were closing on one another now, some of the phantom ridges in the eyes of both youths beginning to materialize into solid-looking shapes. The two worlds were sliding together, like the split images from a film projector move towards union as they are focused on a screen. The landscape was obviously blurred at the edges — many changes had taken place between their separate existences, but the core of the hills darkened into denseness. The perception and depth of their time-separated surroundings began to take on meaning.

The wind is blowing towards the landbridge, thought Esk. If I set the forest alight the fire will cut them off before they get

176

to the rock shelter. My people can escape to the beaches. They'll smell the flames and fly from the invading dwarves.

He stepped into the clearing without further hesitation and staggered towards one of the domestic fires. He would need something to start the wildfire: there would be fat-impregnated blankets in the cave for that. Beneath the trees, inside the forest, the ground was dry and the lower branches leafless. They would ignite quite easily and would soon increase into an irresistible and unquenchable throat of flame that would swallow all before it, even green and damp foliage. Esk had seen it happen before and he knew what could happen if a fire like that got a hold. The Mother's face would be black with anger and Her forest children, the animals, driven in panic-stricken flights over cliffs and headlong into walls of rock. But he could see no alternative He was too weak to run and warn his people, even with the added strength of Richard's nearness.

"Who's that?" cried the crone, her blunt face cocked towards the tree-tops.

Esk ignored her, walking past. She reached out to grasp at him and he struck her forehead hard with his elbow. She spun round once and fell to the floor, apparently unconscious.

He entered the cave and began gathering some skins that lay just inside. As he looked into the darkness of the interior he stiffened. Something was in there!

"Who's there?" he shouted foolishly, his voice distorted with pain, and then realized he had given himself away.

What is it? asked Richard. *Man or beast?*

He explored Esk's mind and found him as ignorant as himself.

A shape shuffled out of the gloomy interior and stood before the caveboy. It was one of Esk's previous captors – a tough-looking dwarf-man. In his hand he grasped a stone axe like a hammer. The fingers were too short to meet around the thick handle.

The two humans stared at one another in the dim light and Esk felt his time to die had arrived too soon.

"No need to come to me now," he said to the ghosts dancing

before him. "No need to bring my soul companion to my side. I am finished."

"No!" shouted Richard, startling both Levan and Kariyos with the violence of the word.

"What is it with the boy?" whispered Kariyos to Levan, who was driving along a ridge with extreme care because of the many rocks that threatened the underside of the vehicle with damage.

"Leave him," said Levan. He did not look at Richard, possibly because he was afraid of seeing a maniac with twisted features and wild eyes were his son should be sitting. Richard squirmed in the seat.

"Get there quickly, Dad. Quickly!"

"Where, for God's sake?"

"Keep going – keep going. I can feel him getting stronger all the time. That way – too much! Yes, now. Keep going."

Levan did as he was told.

The stranger shivered under Esk's scrutiny and his physique underwent a transformation, beginning with his face which rippled like a reflection in a windblown puddle. The eyes took on an intrinsic intelligence. The shadows deepened in the cheeks and the free hand became expressive.

"Richard?" questioned the Neanderthal.

The eyes peered into Esk's as if trying to probe below the exterior: searching the youth's face for signs of an alien presence within. Esk felt Richard coming through strongly and he relaxed his hold on his body allowing his soul brother to assume complete control.

Pain assailed Richard from every corner of Esk's head. When he moved the jaw it came in waves of black and scarlet.

"Who's that?" he asked, using a stranger's vocal cords for the first time. The voice sounded liquid: richer than his own.

"This is Leidermann, Richard. You've got to get away from here. Get your Paleolithic youth to the other end of the island. Hide. There's going to be killing and . . . and God knows what!"

"How did you . . .?" began Richard. His nostrils burned with hot breath.

"Never mind that — do as I say," he snapped back. "It was deliberate," he added, as if Richard at least deserved some explanation. "There's another amongst those that have gone to the Kyrenia rock shelter. He wants to be sure of a few bodies. He feels . . . look, this is wasting time. I've warned you — it's the best I can do."

The Neanderthal dashed into the line of trees and disappeared from view. Behind Richard the old woman groaned.

Richard flashed urgent thoughts to Esk — who appeared to remain single-minded. Fire was the answer. It would warn his people and possibly aid their escape.

"What's the matter with him?" asked Kariyos. Richard heard the words as he returned to his own time, the kinaesthesis causing him to twitch and jerk as senses flooded into the lolling flesh. He could smell the dusty dryness of the air through the open hatch.

The slider had stopped and his father was leaning over him.

"I'm all right," said Richard. His voice sounded listless but he knew that his rate of recovery accelerated logarithmically and that shortly he would be fully sensible.

His father nodded, "You gave us a bit of a scare. We'll have to walk from here anyway — the going's too rough for the slider."

Richard looked out. They were on a slope covered in large boulders. The sweepers on the slider would not be able to cope with those. At the top of the slope was a small escarpment with a ruff of thick bushes. Familiarity soaked into Richard's brain. It was not that he recognized the place by sight. Was it something to do with the touch of the earth below his feet? The angle of the sun? Or the rough compatibility of the superimposed scenery with the "real" rockforms? It was none of these, for the latter needed Esk's eyes to be resting on the same ridge or hollow as Richard's to form any kind of liaison point between past and future. The sun was not the same sun in time or space and the dust had grown upon the land in thick layers — stolen by denudation agents from the hatchet faces of the mountains.

It was none of these.

It was his feeling of a union with his soul-brother. Esk was in him, he was in Esk. They were not just close — spiritually — they were one. A unit. The feeling of power was like fire funnelled through his veins.

Esk threw the torch into the fat-soaked blanket lying in the undergrowth and watched in boyish delight as they flared, the flames clawing their way upwards branch by branch. Climbing to the light above.

The wind rushed in below, filling the pockets where the fire had eaten away the oxygen.

Trees danced red and yellow as the ghosts of the future looked on.

Richard was apart from the other two, standing near an old chainbucket well, when the shot rang out. Kariyos fell to the ground, his shoulder spurting blood.

"The cave!" shouted Levan, frozen in a standing position. A second shot hummed inside a cloud of dust. Levan ran, flung himself, and moulded his body around a rock. Richard fell, shaking, into the shallow rut left by the oxen that had drawn a circle around the well. He waited for a bullet. None came his way.

Instead, another sparked from the rock to which his father clung in the comic adhesive pose of a sunning lizard.

A large man appeared from behind the bushes, seemingly vomited from solid stone. He held a sobbing girl by the hair, a gun at her temple.

Rosemary!

Cautiously, he dragged her towards the slider, his eyes on Levan and Kariyos.

Kariyos stirred and moaned and Levan, unable to hold his position, slid slowly to the ground. Richard could see the terror

180

in his father's face. He knew his father was horrified that the gun might explode against Rosemary's head.

"Don't shoot," whispered Levan hoarsely.

The man stopped and turned slightly, showing Richard the brutality in his big-boned face. Short black hair sprung like coarse grass from his heavy head and a white ball of spittle was caught in the corner of the sullen mouth. The hand holding Rosemary shook her roughly, the gun jabbing against her forehead. A message. *One more movement and the gun will be fired.*

Richard held his breath. The indications pointed towards the man having not noticed him hiding in the rut. If the man had not seen him he must remain perfectly still. There was only thirty yards between them and the shock of suddenly sighting a third person might precipitate a reflex action.

Rosemary would die.

The wind changed and Esk suddenly found himself being confronted by a wall of fire. For a second he stood, like Levan had stood, immobilized by a danger his senses had recognized but his brain had not yet analysed. Then he turned and ran, the roaring monster on his heels.

"Help me!" he cried aloud to his soul-mate, and the pain in his jaw made his head spin in agony.

Come to me! cried Richard silently. *I need your strength and skill!*

The kidnapper was nearing the slider, his back now towards Richard. A tethering staff with a metal collar protruded from the wooden mechanism of the water-drawing machinery. Richard withdrew it from its well-worn socket.

The fire! screamed Esk. It eats me! It eats me!

Me! Me!

I am lost. The Mother takes me to Her breast.

To me! Now!

181

Esk left the sharpness of the pain behind. For the last few seconds of his mortal life he anchored his feet in a wide stance and pulled back on a roughly hewn javelin. His target's head was stark and black against the blue background. Was this his test? Was the Mother offering manhood before death after all?

"*Kill him!*" cried his soul-brother.

The missile was launched, a shining sunbleached wooden shaft that seemed to hang in the sky at the height of its trajectory. Then it fell, metal-tip first and struck its human target behind the right ear with the sound of a catapulted pebble striking a tree-trunk.

"Hooooraaaoo!" shouted the manhunter. Then there was the feeling of drifting like a white seed on the wind. Peace. Tranquillity. A son moving to his Mother's side.

Remember me! was the last thought which passed between himself and the Other. Not the words, but the poignant feeling of not wanting to die, completely.

14

Levan found one of the search parties and called the nearest hospital on a police transmitter. Then he raced back to the cave to await its coming.

Richard was kneeling beside Kariyos placing pads made of shirt material against the old man's wound. The bullet had smashed the left clavicle and blood soaked into the pads, and through, within minutes. Rosemary was sitting, crying to herself, some feet away.

"Don't remove the old pads, son. Just put new ones on top." Kariyos's eyes were closed. His face an ugly white.

"I know," Richard replied.

Levan nodded. He walked quickly over to the body of the kidnapper. There was a huge lump above and behind the right ear. Split skin had allowed a trickle of blood to trace a passage down the side of the neck. Fighting down the contents of his stomach Levan picked up the thick wrist and felt for the pulse. He dropped it quickly, sensing the deadness in the clammy skin.

My son has killed a man! The thought was not so much shocking, as unreal.

Looking across at Richard, he expected to see something unusual about him — but the youth displayed no external differences, nothing to indicate that any dramatic change had taken place within him either. A sound came from overhead and Levan realized the hospital had sent a skyhopper. He turned his attention to more practical things.

Later, when Kariyos was safely on his way. Levan again considered his two charges. Rosemary had refused to go to the hospital to be treated for mild shock — insisting that she was perfectly well. She wanted Levan to drive her home in the slider and not wanting to upset her further he and the hopper medics succumbed to her fierce entreaties.

She now sat, in a dishevelled and grubby state, staring at the youth who had killed her captor (whose body had also been removed along with Kariyos). Two policemen stood, a little way off, keeping a respectable distance until Levan indicated that they could carry out their interviews. They seemed in no hurry. He called them now and they briefly questioned the three of them. The majority of the enquiries were directed at Rosemary, who was finally vociferous only with her tears. Levan was pleased that they did not linger too long on the actual killing, although Richard outwardly appeared undisturbed by his part in the event. Eventually the police were satisfied but pointed out that it was by no means the end of the affair. Normal legal proceedings would have to take their course. Levan said he understood.

"We're even now," said Rosemary, after the police had left.

Richard gave her a small, tight smile.

Now what the hell was all that about?

The boy turned to him.

"He's gone, Dad. I think . . . I think he died. There was a fire . . . Anyway, he's not in me any longer. I feel . . . I feel a bit empty now."

Thank God, he thought. The boy has come out of it at last. Shock treatment?

"Are you sure he's gone?" he asked.

"Positive. He just sort of . . . faded or something. He was afraid, and then, after he threw the spear – he was jubilant. Afraid, but elated too, if that doesn't sound silly."

Levan said quickly, "It sounds how it should. He? He threw the spear? This caveboy?"

Let him work it out of his system for good. Maybe it will never come back? Some schizophrenics are cured. Some.

Richard's anxious look disappeared, to be replaced by a glower.

"You don't believe me. You *still* don't believe me. You're

incredible, Dad. How do you think I threw the pole? I haven't the skill or the strength. Look at the distance. . . ."

"I believe you Richard," replied Rosemary, her chin propped on her knees.

He nodded at her absently and then looked back towards his father.

Levan threw up his hands.

"Look, Richard, please. I love you . . ." Richard winced ". . . You're my son. But I can't accept what I know to be impossible, can I? I could easily lie to you. . . ."

"You just tried to – but I saw it in your face."

"Well . . . that proves I can't do it. I'm a practical man, Richard."

"But that other man was there too. Leidermann. He was there, in a Neanderthal's body. He spoke to me. Warned me."

Levan shook his head. "Leidermann left yesterday – for the States."

Richard shouted, "I bet he's lying somewhere in some hotel – out cold. His mind isn't with him. It's back in Pleistocene times."

"Look, Richard. See my side of it," Levan said. "If you be-lieved you'd been transported back to the Old Stone Age then your mind could fabricate other things. Like Leidermann's voice."

Richard looked up. "So it doesn't matter what I say?"

His father shook his head sadly.

Suddenly Richard stiffened in his arms and broke away.

"I've just thought! The cave. I wrote on the wall of the cave . . ."

"You what?" asked Levan. *What was the crazy kid up to now? He said he had never been here before.*

"In Esk's body – *then*! I painted my name on the wall of the cave using the Shaman's red ochre. I think that's the colour I used. Anyway, you can match the age of the paints – you'll see I was there." He turned to Rosemary.

"The paintings – you must have seen them."

She shook her head doubtfully. "It was very dark. And wet."

"Wet?" questioned Levan.

"Yes — the water was running down the walls."

Levan sighed. "Must be an underground spring, Richard."

The youth looked at his father.

"Let's go and see — we can only go and see. They might be there!"

They took a light from the slider and investigated but the walls were blank. Levan guessed that limestone had been deposited over the pictures — if there ever had been any there. Anyway, they'd gone, and with them Richard's proof of his journey.

"I'm sorry Richard," he said, his voice echoing around the cave.

"Well, if you dig here," said the boy, "you'll probably make yourself at least some small change in artifacts." He kicked the dirt floor with his foot.

"I doubt it," said Levan.

"Why?" asked the other two in unison.

"Because, if you look carefully, you'll see dips in the floor and there are piles of earth outside the cave. They're covered in brown weeds now but the dirt came from in here. It's been well dug already — I know the signs. Now. Let's get you home, Rosemary. Your mother will have heard the news by now and she'll be wondering why I haven't rushed you back."

They went outside and climbed into the slider. Rosemary's eyes were ringed with the black marks of sleeplessness, and her face looked white and drawn, but the sobbing fit was over, and the nervous jerky movements she had displayed, on breaking away from the dead man's grasp, were beginning to lessen. It was better to take her back to Loraine like this than as she had been immediately after her rescue.

There was an emotional reunion at the bungalow during which Levan called the Morphou hospital to enquire about Kariyos. The old man wasn't in good shape but he wasn't dangerously ill. Levan hoped his heart was strong enough to carry him through.

Then he took Richard back to the Akrotiri hospital and delivered him up to the nurses, apologizing for taking the boy away but saying he felt it had done some good.

"Getting to be a habit," said the sister, ushering Richard into his room. "We'll see what the doctor has to say tomorrow."

Levan winked at his son, who murmured to him, "It'll be all right now. I'm sorry Esk got killed though – in the fire."

"It was a long time ago, son."

Richard stared into his eyes, and said slowly, "Yes, I suppose it was."

On the way back to the bungalow Levan decided to repurchase Esk's bones if he could get them. He wanted to bury the boy again, secretly, somewhere in the hills. It didn't matter where, so long as Richard knew his . . . his what? His friend? . . . so long as the Paleolithic boy was safe from future bounty hunters.

The red evening sun peered through a space between two mountains – as if watching Levan's movements from behind a cracked wall. An eye on my progress, he thought. Funny, when Richard was complaining of pains in his body that morning at the hospital, the boy had kept rubbing, almost unconsciously, the second finger of his left hand; as if he had an irritation there. Levan remembered something he had recorded in his notes on the skeletons. The smallest of them had had a metacarpal fracture. It was on that finger. Richard could have noticed it before, of course, when he had been helping to label the bones. The point was, he had not deliberately drawn Levan's attention to it, as he had the pains in his jaw. Levan did not want to believe in quasi-scientific or supernatural occurrences, but he wanted to play safe – like those primitive tribes of early-Christian Africa, accepting a new belief but retaining the essentials of the old pagan religions, blending them. He would bury the bones in Cyprus, if only to salve a nagging doubt.

"Then you can stop watching me," he said aloud to the sun, realizing he was addressing the wrong deity. That was a much later form of worship.

There was much he still did not understand and into which

he did not care to delve too deeply. There was the long, triumphant howl that belonged to a dog's throat – but which Richard had used after the killing. There was Richard's face, the canine expression shattering like glass immediately after the howl. There was the sense of loss that showed in Richard's bearing too.

Loraine was waiting for him when he arrived back at her bungalow and she folded herself around him as he entered the room.

"Thanks for bringing her home."

"It wasn't me, you know. It was Richard."

"Or someone," she said.

He drew back and flicked her hair away from her eyes. "Not you too?" he asked.

"Of course. I'm one of the true believers. You know where Alan is?"

He said, "I'm not interested."

"Interested or not, I'll tell you. He's in Turkey. He called me. Said that he was inside one of the Neanderthals and they were heading towards the Black Sea. He's rented a house there, so that he can lie where he falls, when his mind leaves his body, without being disturbed. . . ."

Levan's stomach turned over.

"That's dangerous – what if he was – well, doing something, with fire, or in the bath . . .?"

"What do you care? You don't believe it."

"I want to stay sane."

She laughed, "Of course, he's the Chief or whatever they called them. He had to be that – Alan couldn't bear to inhabit an unimportant person." There was a moment of quiet.

"When are you going to marry me?" he asked.

"Sometime. We'll talk about it. Later."

Outside the bungalow, the night dropped like a tightly meshed net over the Mediterranean, stars poking through the holes.

15

The disruptive short people had gone — driven out by the fire that had swept them north-eastwards across the island and along its arm. Reng had watched the progress of their camp fires as they had moved along the strip to the continent. The new Shaman of the Gren was glad they had gone, of course, but he wished they had been punished more severely. They had left death in their wake and had scarred his beautiful birthplace with their carelessness.

Now it remained to collect the bodies of the Gren and bury them in the ever-pregnant belly of the Mother. Esk, of course, would be one of those. The land was still smouldering from the blaze, several turns of the fire-eye later. At least the animals would not venture inside the black ring of charred forest yet. The bodies would still be whole. There was Granla to be found, too. And a woman who had been out collecting eggs. Reng would arrange a ritual burial for them all.

An idea took root in his mind. He would give Granla, as the ex-Shaman, a magnificent farewell. Not that he felt any remorse or sadness over Granla's demise — nor indeed over the death of Esk, for which he was directly responsible. The living must live on and Esk could not have remained while Reng was alive. The youth's contention for leadership had been too strong.

If he gave Granla a burial to remember it would place the final seal on Reng's leadership. He could wear the tree-head — could become the stag! Perhaps service several women that night, when he was potent with power and magic? The thought appealed very strongly.

He walked down to shelter from his observation point and called to Leaf.

"Have they gone?" replied the other youth as he answered his Shaman's call.

"Gone? Ah, the Short Ones — yes. Their fires are now far away. Why they did not settle in another part of our birthplace — far from us — will always be a mystery to me."

Leaf nodded. "Many peoples have tried to take this place from us — or so the stories tell. Certainly in my time this is the third group to come. And always they want to fight with the Gren. This is a big place. They could go to the far side and we should never bother each other. But, always, they have to find us out."

"It is natural for us to protect our own shelter," said Reng. "Why can't they leave us alone? Short Ones, Tall Ones, thin ones, fat ones. They always come. I have been thinking — after we bury the Sha . . . after we bury Granla, we shall take the men out onto the arm of the Mother which touches the place where all these people come from."

"Why?"

"To dig. There is a sandy place where the arm is very narrow. We shall dig a channel across the arm — a wide channel, to stop these invaders encroaching upon our place. . . ."

Leaf was looking at his leader in awe. His eyes widened as the idea registered. This was indeed a great Shaman! His counsel with the Mother had already begun.

"Yes, I see it," cried the excited Leaf. "I perceive the water sparkling — on one side our people, safe from aggressors, and on the other the dark shapes of the disappointed ones. I see them turn . . ." his hands made the imagined movements of the would-be enemy reality ". . . and walk with hunched shoulders, thwarted by our glorious plan."

"Our plan?"

"Yours, Shaman," said the nimble-minded Leaf. "Your device, your great channel to protect the Gren. I must tell the others. May I tell the others?" he pleaded.

Reng acquiesced. "You may tell them. You may also order a party to search for any bodies of the Gren which may have been caught in the fire. I have a feeling my brother Esk may have been one of them."

The face before Leaf was without expression. The youth nodded and ran quickly into the ring of men sitting around the largest of the fires. Animatedly and without introduction he began to describe the wonders they were about to perform.

For a while Reng watched him in amusement, then the Shaman wandered down the track to the shore of the sea mother and sat on a rock, looking out over her vast expanse of shining wet skin.

One day, I will cross you too, he thought. There was no boat in his mind. But there was *something* there quite unlike the hollow logs from which the Gren fished. Who knew what it was? An object which had no name inside the head of a man who hardly knew he was a man. Deep within that head, somewhere, were glass and brass instruments for finding ways across water; for pinning suns to skies; for needle-pointing paths through moon-high waves; for pulling stars closer to ask a position. Deeper still inside were journeys tracked in coloured ink on stiff paper – were devices for breaking time into numbered pieces. Deeper yet the finely curled springs, delicate spindles, cogs and wheels – curved and rounded, squared and blocked, scaled, measured and marked, resting on liquid or trained fingers: pulled, pushed, adjusted and set – patterned for pleasure and purpose, precisioned for accuracy, polished and buffed – answering to questioning hands.

Closer, though, out of the dim light of a primitive mind, came a short pointed shaft, loosed from taut gut, and fletched with the feathers of eagles.

The ring of stone on stone sounded in the heart of the Pleistocene day.